THE COLLARED KITTTEN

BELLA DONNA

ROBERT ALEXANDER

First published in 2020 by:
Britain's Next Bestseller
An imprint of
Live It Ventures LTD
126 Kirkleatham Lane, Redcar. Cleveland.
TS10 5DD

Copyright © 2020 Bella Donna and Robert Alexander
The moral right of Bella Donna and Robert Alexander to be identified as the authors of this work has been asserted by them in accordance with the Copyright, Designs and Patents Act 1988.

All rights reserved.

No part of this book may be reproduced or transmitted in any form or any means without written permission from the copyright holder, except by a reviewer who may quote brief passages in connection with a review for insertion in a newspaper, magazine, website, or broadcast.

A catalogue record for this book is available from the British Library.

All characters appearing in this work are fictitious. Any resemblance to real persons, living or dead, is purely coincidental.

www.bnbsbooks.co.uk
@BNBSbooks
Cover design: vikncharlie
Printed in the U.K

'Dedicated to my Son, with love, who is too young to read this yet'

ROBERT ALEXANDER

CHAPTER 1

Tuppence, this is the night — this is your moment, see you at seven.

'Red heels,' she excitedly whispered. 'Spikes!'

They had been placed by the bed along with the sexiest dress she had ever seen - a micro mini red with a scoop back showing the top of her ass.

'How? Did I tell him my size? No...'she whispered to herself and her secret friend, waiting for him to respond.

'Baby girl, he is hooked. He came back while you slept, his fingers traversed your body, each curve measured with his incredibly experienced fingertips. He even licked them, tasted your damp flesh. He couldn't get enough.'

She hugged herself, stretching out within the silk sheets and eye-popping surroundings as she viewed herself in the large mirrored ceiling, smiling at the reflection of her nakedness.

She stroked her fingers over her soft nipples, wanting

to feel them harden. 'Oh Daddy, you would so like to be touching me now, I just know it.'

Letting one hand stray to her pussy, she spread her legs, feeling more and more excited as her flower was exposed in the mirrors.

'I'm gonna have you begging for this pussy, you know you need it,' she said as she slid a finger inside her vagina, feeling her wetness.

'I like you like this,' she said to the voice that whispered in her ear, sometimes bitter... no, always sharp and vicious with a game plan. It had been there for as long as she could remember, and now she was used to its abuse.

The hand is elegant; she thought as she reread his note. She stroked it obsessively and clutched it to her.

'Oh Mister... no, Daddy! I'm going to take you somewhere you will never return from.'

For a girl so wise in life, she was also innocent and naive.

Her father had taught her not to feel, or so he and she believed. He would, in one sentence, call her a princess but finish saying she was the most adept hustler he had ever known. His reasons being that he didn't want his only girl ever to get hurt, and she now believed she was genuinely unassailable.

Moments where her heart felt like it had drowned, she would put that down to empathy for others. Never outside of this realm did she dare ever venture. After all, she felt so much, so surely there was nothing more. Almost seeing herself as part of the earth and not human, she carefully maintained her state of ambivalence to her tragedy and emotional distance to those around her, cosseting all others their surroundings.

The voice would jibe, *'They're bleeding you, you sad fuck!* Nevertheless, she seemed to enjoy it, enjoy being abused.

She had left for London in a hurry. After bed-hopping for a month, she had fallen in with those she considered the 'right types.'

She was tired of those dead beats with whom she was making do and just existing. She wanted -no, damn well deserved - some luxury in her life.

If someone wants me to whore for them, they need to offer more than a wet patch on their old stained bed and some cheap breakfast cereal before I leave. Any man or woman will have to treat me like a queen for me to spread my legs.

'OH, WOW, THE COLLARED KITTEN! I LIKE YOU,' SHE whispered to herself.

The sarcastic vile voice that dogged her, but kept her insanity company, answered.

You will make a killing, you filthy little tramp.

She giggled a little as she approached the dark corner of the Soho street, the postcode desirable and the establishment suitably subtle.

A flash of light beating across the sign where the rest of the club was dark, classy and exclusive.

Speak softly but confidently and act as though they want you, tart. You're used to it; the barbed voice said as she sauntered up to the door.

She flicked her chestnut hair from her face as the

wind picked up, her mini skirt and bra top accentuated her soft curves and tiny waist. Her skinny legs shook a little with the adrenaline she had come to love.

Two granite featured doormen stood with arms folded, not giving her a second glance. She was used to this, or so she thought. She sidled up to them, pretending to fish in her purse for something.

Still, they would not budge.

'I'm Crystal,' she haughtily stated, as if expecting to be welcomed like a Hollywood celebrity. She sighed. 'Goodness, I have no particular invitation, but I did complete an application form and was told just to turn up.'

Still nothing.

They stared through her like she was nothing more than street trash. Their muscles flexed in their short sleeves, so she ventured, 'Aren't you cold?'

She went to stroke one of their arms but was pushed back firmly, gently. 'No need miss, your admission is secured, and no, we are not cold.'

The other one laughed. 'A better question for you, with the lack of clothing. There was no need,' he finished condescendingly and gestured for her to enter.

Blushing, she stuck her nose in the air and entered. She heard them click and speak on their mics as she approached the receptionist, elegant but dressed, with nothing but a collar about her neck to show any pizazz.

She gave the two security men a knowing look. 'Oh hey, no coat or anything? You're either poor or incredibly stupid.'

The paranoia beat its way to the front of Crystal's

mind as she remembered stealing the clothes on Oxford Street.

Top Shop was so easy, she thought, but even still she shifted about in the top and skirt, wondering if they knew.

The receptionist was blonde with a sexy chignon and toyed with her collar.

Fucking plain bitch! I'm not intimidated!

But Crystal began to wonder if she had had the wrong idea about this place. She hovered at a dark wooden door, not sure if she should run and save face or make an idiot of herself as usual.

It was so understated, sheer elegance with lowlights casting shadows on dark walls. Nothing like she had expected, but then surely, this was London - no need for bells and whistles.

Nervously, she pulled at her skirt again and tried to stand tall. The receptionist was laughing with the security and got up to open the door. 'Honestly, it's just a bit of fun. You will do just fine.'

Crystal wondered if the collar was part of the club or just the receptionist's little fetish. Still, she liked it. It was sexy, excellent quality leather and very snug around the receptionist's long slim neck.

The slinky girl hinted with her elegant hand that Crystal should enter and made her realise she had stared for far too long, dissecting her with her eyes and curious mind. She smiled bitterly, furious with herself but turned as instructed, at which point the girl fobbed near the door, and they glided open.

Immediately Crystal absorbed the sultry atmosphere

and low, thumping beat of the club. She felt more at ease and let the music bounce in and around her.

A long corridor, with vintage dancing girl pictures and some sort of Arabic scripture, led to two lavishly decorated red doors. Her hand was shaking as she pushed through them gently, the music filling her body until she thought it would burst.

The sights amazed her, the smell of sweaty bodies lusting after each other tantalising her senses. Her blood pumped fiercely around her body, making her pulse pound everywhere a girl would want it to.

CHAPTER 2

The Collared Kitten was everything she had dared to imagine as the bitter satanic voice enjoyed crushing her dreams.

You're just a sad fuck existing on pipe dreams and fuck you; I do love fucking with them. I set you up consistently, sweet cheeks, and you can never be rid of me.

Still trembling, she lifted her head so as not to appear shy or new to such things. Always show them confidence, even when you think you haven't got a chance, Princess.

She loved the way her father always called her Princess, and she always tried to live up to his words.

Head high, look straight ahead, never look back. Hold their gaze and never stare at the floor, remember that sweetheart. I love you

'Where are you?' she whispered to the voice. 'What do I do?' But she couldn't hear.

The low grinding music pulsated and, as she took a

deep breath, about to turn and run, the sensuous figure of a raven-haired Collared Kitten girl came close and reached for her hand,

'There you are…?'

Crystal smiled nervously. 'Crystal – how could you forget?'

The girl laughed. 'Oh, I never forget, Miss. I just wondered if you had changed your name yet again. Such is the life of an escapee?'

The last part of what she said was lost on Crystal, as the vixen's soft hand pulled her forward into the dazzling atmosphere and gestured her to the bar that undulated with the sea of hot, horny bodies, thirsty for everything.

'A drink? On me, get rid of those nerves you're feeling?' She tapped the bar, and a young bartender left all others to see to her.

'Give her a grey goose, and if she wants more you're not to refuse, just make sure she's sensible enough, you know? Her reactions? They're integral, so you see this is my little star for the night and oh my, won't Mister be pleased with me.' She winked at the bartender.

'Go on then, drink,' she said as Crystal fingered the glass. 'And when you're ready, we could use some entertainment.'

She showed her the floor. Crystal's eyes alighted on the cages. Some were glass with tiny breathing holes, with one she loved especially. It was like a birdcage, and her heartbeat quickly as the dark-haired girl smiled, stroking her head and touching her face.

'Such a pretty one. If you want the birdcage, you'll have to earn it and see off all pretenders.'

She pointed to where two girls danced erotically together. 'See, them two? They want the cage too, and when they're done seeing off all the competition, they'll see each other. I got to go now, sweets. You have one in particular that you need to impress tonight?'

With a sharp change in her expression, she glared at Crystal and stated for clarity. 'Just one.'

She went to leave but turned coyly to face her again. 'Oh, damn it! I nearly forgot, I've got to introduce you to someone, actually something, before I leave you to your liquid doughnut.' She winked and stroked Crystal's waist. 'I'm pretty sure you work out regularly, like, so sweet girl, deep breath. It's just a little quirk we have residing.'

She coughed as she shared a look with the bartender, who replied, 'Perp you mean?'

She stifled a giggle. 'Put those drinks to the side. I'm pretty sure she'll be back.'

He lined up the drinks at the back of the bar as a redhead twenty-something nervously sat there and two Tom Cats, male clients in tow, whispered to Crystal's companion.

'Was he bought in? Looks a bit lost.'

The girl leaned closer to them as Crystal strained to hear. 'Yes, and is no concern of yours. You just see to your gentlemen!'

She covered quickly what she was about to say as the Tom Cat's dates for the night became curious. 'Nothing to concern you sweet things. Enjoy your night fellas.'

The two Toms took the hint and led their clients away. She looked frustratedly after them, then softened, turning to Crystal and taking her hand.

Crystal's eyes had wandered up to a large window with heavy curtains that was above the bar. They opened slightly, just as she was about to look away.

An austere face with sharp angular features stared back at her... through her. The girl laughed and pulled Crystal's face away. 'That's management, sweets. That's as close as you get to the top! Though what he paid for that luxury, shows on his face, you reckon?'

They both shuddered simultaneously as they looked away and Crystal's companion led her quickly through the heaving, grinding and highly sexual atmosphere of the club.

She stopped outside an indiscriminate booth and twitched the curtain.

'You decent?' Then rolled her eyes. 'Best make yourself then, I have a project for you.'

She pulled the curtains tight behind her.

'Now listen here, honey, this is integral. Beyond these fine drapes is an odd little man, sycophant, of whom I'm sure you've met and disregarded as many have before, as disgusting and not worthy, hmm? But he is a requirement. I want you to answer anything he asks you with absolute honesty. Transparency is important at this stage; you get it? He will want to see what you have got and how you use it, so no shy little girl act, show him whatever and more.'

She winked seductively at Crystal before carrying on.

'Oh, but don't let him touch you. Ugh, such a purvy little creature, but what else would you expect of Babylon, hey? And don't look so nervous, baby, he won't bite, and if he did, you'd thank us for putting you down, as I swear, he's riddled with every disease there is!'

She took Crystal's trembling hand. 'Go on tiger, momma watching over you ok?'

Spellbound by the girl's constant sweet and soft manner, Crystal brushed past her, wanting to feel her skin again, her eyes penetrating Sadie. The latter tapped her ass and giggled, leaving her to it as she entered the booth.

It was elegant, but with a stale stench of sweat, the sides of the couch wrapped the seat giving privacy to whoever sat there. Opposite the deep curved leather couch was a spotlighted small stage area. In front of the couch was a low dark wooden table with a half-finished drink on it.

As Crystal slowly moved towards the couch, a stubby fingered hand reached for the glass.

'For fuck sake, get on stage so I can see what the fuck you look like! Christ sakes, or are you another little fucking madam who wants to waste my time?' The voice was harsh but not strong.

Crystal slowly and nervously moved towards the stage, trying to see who was talking. A dwarfed bald unshaven male sat slumped on it; his feet crossed on the table. He stared at Crystal, looking her up and down.

'Hmm, nice tits, come on darling hurry up and mount that stage.' She took a deep breath and stood up straight and worked her ass as she walked, knowing she had danced for scum like this in her past.

This place is meant to be different, though. I can do this, just like old times, but it's got to be my best work, Crystal honey. You want this bad.

She climbed the stage and turned to face the decrepit dwarf. The lights were far too bright for the small raised platform he called a stage and that she now teetered on. Minutes passed before she felt that weird confidence she loved and went from awkward to fuck you, I'm all fucking that.

'Hi, I'm Crystal.' Silence greeted her. 'Here for the audition.' She attempted to get a reply of some kind. 'What would you like to see?'

She heard him fidgeting on the couch before he replied, 'Your pussy. How about you flash me your fucking snatch, huh? No? Ok then, show me why you're here you whore. DANCE! For fucks sake! Do you know how to dance, bitch?'

She felt humiliated, but it didn't last long, He hides behind the lights, I can deal with this slimy cunt.

'Music?' she aggressively said, as she heard him wanking.

'Wanna lollipop too?' he snarled. 'You need to be drip-fed everything for fuck sake? Just fucking move your whore snatch for me will ya? Show me why you should be collared.'

She cleared her throat and started rubbing her thighs sensuously. She could hear him enjoying it, and even though she despised him, things like this always got her hot. Most who knew her said she had the attitude of an erotic dancer as part of her soul. They had to find it hot, no matter who was watching and oozed down her thighs.

'You're going to have to do more than this to stay here, whore. What are you willing to show the clients? Some stuck-up little Mummy's girl cunt? Or are you gonna impress me and will you dance for our clients like the filthy little slut you need to be?'

She was shocked at his bluntness, but also found it sexually exciting. She knew what she had to do; this wasn't the first club she had whored herself out at, but this one was different and sophisticated, which meant comfort and luxuries.

'I ...' she began.

The dwarf was not gonna wait for her. 'Shut the fuck up and show me. I've seen better cunts then you, so you better pick this up, or you can walk!'

She started working her body, touching herself, grinding her hips to the imaginary music which she now moved up a beat.

'The Collared Kitten clients are number 1. They take care of their chosen Kittens. So, whore, is there anything you would refuse them?'

This question was asked clearly, and Crystal felt the importance. Now was not the time to be unsure or prudish. 'Nothing I won't do for them, but you can fuck off,' she replied, regretting showing her repulse of him.

She heard him laugh at her and felt it was a good sign, so decided to tease him more and let him do whatever he wanted.

She pulled her top down just enough and threw her head back, stroking her erect nipples.

'Fuck!' she heard as the top slipped and her full-size C breasts were exposed. It got her hot, and she wanted to feel him, wondered what his cock would feel like inside her. It made her move dirtier, sluttier. Used to playing for any crowd in a club, her wetness began to drive her wild, wanting to stroke herself for him. Thoughts raced through her mind of him eating her pussy. Her soaked panties were visible, and her supple thighs looked beautiful as they shone with her cum.

She exposed herself, lowering to the floor and thrusting her body up, hearing him groan and pull on his cock.

Had he cum already? Fuck, that was quick, but then I'm a hot hoochie momma, and no one can resist.

She bristled with pride until the vicious voice brought her crashing back to earth.

It's not him, is it? Fuck's sake are you desperate.

It laughed bitterly, but she recovered and dismissed it.

Fuck off you pathetic cunt.

She was too caught up in the moment to take notice. Her body began to sweat as she moved faster and more erotically. She heard him cumming as her fingers dipped into her knickers and she orgasmed hard, running them up to her breasts.

'Fucking touch me then you pervert!' she cried out as her pussy throbbed wildly.

He got up and slowly walked to the stage, rubbing his shrunken penis through a mass of unkempt pubic hair and cum-covered fingers. He stood staring, from Crystal's excited hot face to her wet panties and then to the curtain door, her fingers still playing and fingering herself. She needed this job and decided she would let him fuck her to get it.

Maybe that's the key? Perhaps he secretly fucks you, the kinky cunt, and then hires… like a bit of danger, do you? You sad little fuck!

She eyed him sensuously and becoming demanding, growled. 'Touch my pussy for me, lick me!'

She teased more, pulling her panties aside to show her smooth wet vagina, his eyes bulged, and his undersized cock begin to harden.

As he reached out desperate to finger her, he stopped sharply, a look of sheer horror on his face, the colour drained. Standing at the curtain was the manager she had seen earlier that night from the office window. Not a word was said, but the atmosphere had been sucked out and replaced by a vacuum.

Her eyes briefly flicked over him, but she had to look away, her primal defence kicking in. Never once did he return her gaze, but she felt his eyes penetrating. His stare was targeted viciously at the dwarf, burning him with those dark red eyes, watching him squirm and move quickly back to the leather couch.

He stared at the floor, trying to zip his cock away and answered her venomously.

'I'm not allowed, you filthy fucking slut! But you're hired, now fuck off outta my sight.'

Crystal got to her feet and looked over to the curtain. No one was there, and the curtain was closed.

She questioned herself for a moment. Had the manager been there, seconds before?

Shuddering, she climbed off the stage watching the dwarf take a filthy hankie out of his pocket and wipe his cum fingers and then his mouth.

She stopped in front of him, lifted her skirt and sorted her panties comfortably over her pussy. She knew, although his head stayed down, he was desperate to look at her again, and was disappointed that she couldn't tease him enough to do so. Nevertheless, she skipped past, disgusted with herself knowing she had just cum over the filthy cunt.

The club was heaving with bodies sweating and enjoying each other, she felt an adrenaline rush through her veins, making her yearn for more action, and she knew she'd get it.

I'm more elegant than any of them bitches.

She returned to the bar, feeling molested by the perverted little man's attention and noticed there was one booth with black silk curtains lit by tiny candles. It was guarded by two girls who wore red skimpy bikini type costumes, long tails and devils' horns finished the look and a club collar of course. Although incredibly sexual, they were imposing, and she found them more attractive for it.

She wanted to touch them, lick them, rub herself against their hard bodies.

She wanted to tease them and make them angry with her so she could see what they'd do.

Her breath caught in her throat as he entered.

Robert Alexander dressed in subtle designer

elegance with chiselled features and devilish good looks. A path cleared as he approached the booth, the girl's bent over in front of him, and he tapped each on the ass. They lifted back the curtains for him to enter, clapping their hands in unison as a drink was immediately placed in front of him.

At no time did he need to ask for anything or even acknowledge anyone.

She saw him gesture for the curtains to be left open, her mouth dry as she gulped back the grey goose and tapped for more. The bartender lined them up. 'Pretty sure you'll need more than a couple,' he laughed and left her with a line of four.

Her eyes wandered up as the office curtains closed. She hadn't meant to look up; those eyes just stole away any good feeling. Looking around the floor, she noticed there were 14 booths, each made with a curved high-backed leather seat with a table and a curtain that could be pulled across the front.

Three booths, one of which was Robert Alexander's, were set with black silk curtains and appeared slightly bigger than the others.

The two dancing girls had moved closer to her, their dancing so erotic that most now watched and cleared tables. She snaked up to them, feverishly excited by the attention and letting the music move her, feeling the pump and grind until her body acted on its own.

That insane confidence filled her again and made her single people out and perform solely for them. It was intensely arousing and the control she felt made her moves erotic and bold, knowing she could pick the pockets of the wealthy just so. Her two companions were intoxicating, initially, but soon she grew tired of how they hung on her and milked her for attention.

Fiercely she owned the scene though she would realise much later that they were products of a larger machine.

I'll never be a sado like them. I'm the one who's lusted after. They're just thieves, trying to get in on my action.

Weak-willed men are easy pickings for you, you filthy hot slut. She loved the confidence that the voice in her head often gave her and replied, *you cunt,* knowing it would enjoy her downfall yet again.

But I'll enjoy myself all the same.

CHAPTER 3

SHE SCANNED THE THUMPING PRIMITIVE SCENE OF HOT bodies wanting and having each other.

Sophistication echoed everywhere. This was no cheap joint for hookers - these girls were carefully selected for their unique qualities. As she thoroughly and lustfully inspected each scene, she became even more intoxicated. She knew this place would become addictive.

Her body ached at the sexual tension, the men controlling their girls with chains on collars, their hands feasting on the different bodies and kinks.

Two girls surrounded one man, their bodies oiled and painted. He arched back at their attentions. His neck was being fiercely eaten by one as the other ripped at his shirt and trousers, her tongue driving him wild as she traced lines down his body to his cock.

Some girls gave the meanest head she had ever seen. She saw one guy cum so hard that one of the club's

Kittens had to restrain him as his hands were too tight on the girl's throat. The security was strong, so hot, they were imposing but not muscular, and they controlled by dominating. The one who had intervened soothed the savage guy who looked like he'd kill the girl. That took grit, class and qualities born into you.

Rubbing herself up against the two dancing girls to further entice her growing crowd, she pressed herself against the dark-haired girl's back, licking her neck and burying herself in her hair. Her hands slipped down her body, brushing her aroused nipples as the girl's head rolled back in ecstasy.

She had always been bi-curious with a few very minor lesbian liaisons - just cuddling naked, brushing each other's hair and some curious touching, but had never tried lesbian loving before.

Now she wanted it.

She wanted to put these girls in their place and own the club. After that dwarfed pervert, she needed this. Whether she dominated both or let them fuck her, she knew she wanted to be number one in the client's eyes.

This is my crowd. Her hands were travelling up the girl's thigh. Her friend was looking stunned—my flock.

Crystal laughed to herself again. It had been the blonde who had been trying to steal attention from her. Trying to get off on my show? Now, look at you, more suited to the slab or a butcher's block…

'I'm not jealous, you know,' she whispered to herself. 'Just toxic.'

She wanted to be sexed by them, but they just took.

Selfish sad bitches, you're not for that pretty cage tonight.

Ha, I laugh coz you're not natural enough. You want it too bad whereas I just want fucking sex.

The dark-haired girl's wetness glistened under the lights as Crystal toyed in and out of her expectant lips. The dancer gasped and fell back onto her – she laughed as the girl scrambled away, leaving her in the shadow of Robert Alexander, further, to be known as 'Daddy.' But for now, as she slowly stared up at him, she saw why she had become so passionate, determined to fuck him and knew that he had been watching her the minute he had walked into the nightclub.

It was fear mixed with deep primitive arousal, and she loved it.

She caught her breath as he held out his hand. She had noticed him subconsciously as darkness all night, and she had been spellbound.

'And that was for me?' His voice was soft but arrogant and so hot on her ears.

Soft 'civi' fingers wrapped around her wrist and pulled her to her feet. She fell into him, and after he had let her feel his hard-on, he pushed her back keeping a tight grip on her wrist.

'Dominant little thing aren't you!' he said, letting her feel his manhood for just a second longer.

Nervously she looked around trying to catch her breath, 'For you? I've not seen you before now, Mister?' she spluttered, trying to pull her arm away and winced as his grip didn't release. Although he wasn't hurting her, she did struggle.

'Do you want me to let you go?' he toyed with her, he appeared so dark. His eyes were blue but looked black, his perfect manicure never once grazed her even if she wanted it to.

She could not answer; her tongue felt huge in her mouth, idiot!

'You should not be on the floor yet, Kitten, you have not been collared,' he said with sarcasm. 'But that's fine, your collar has already been tagged to me.'

She did not understand the tagging.

What the fuck? And who the fuck are you?

She glanced around at other Kittens, all with elegant leather collars with a small bell by the throat and a black fob next to it. Some of them had a silver name tag inside the bell.

Is that what he is referring to? Oh god, his grip on my waist is so hot! Oh yeah, he's desperate, sad coz I'm a natural, not like the other fake bitches.

'No that's not what I see.' He answered her thoughts which further shook her. 'Do you want to know what I see?'

He pulled her to a stool pushing her onto it, stroking her thighs as he made her sit, his fingers touching her wet panties and slit. She naturally opened her legs wider, there was no faking it, and it infuriated her how her body was betraying her.

For fucks sake I'm hot for it with him. I gotta control, I can't let him think I'm easy or some desperate cunt.

He laughed, pushing her thighs back together and pulling down her skirt. 'You're quite an eyeful, aren't you? Or is that all fakery?' He stroked her face.

'No need to answer – it's funny. I enjoy a bit of fakery yet here you are natural apart from a bit of makeup. Still, there's no sin in vanity, because that's what it blatantly is, hmm? You think you're so fine, don't you, Miss?'

Crystal snatched his hand away clawing at it with her sharpened pointed nails,

'Fake enough for you?' she haughtily said as her talons tore at his flesh.

'Oh ouch!' he mocked and held his soft hand to his mouth, 'Want to taste?' he said as he put it to hers, the blood oozing over his fine shirt and suit.

Her full pink lips trembled as she smelled his blood and cologne mix, she wanted it, wanted to taste him. Just a lick, but the overpowering urge became too much as she softly took his hand and sucked and tongued where the blood oozed. Eyeing him, she knew where to look, the veins on his neck protruded, and his eyes betrayed him as her sucking became harder. The blood in her veins turned to ice. What was it she saw?

Why did she feel like she was about to die? Every pulse in her body, beat out a fierce rhythm as he let her suck him more, she wanted to stop, but the voice in her head urged her on, wouldn't let her finish.

She sobbed as he pulled his hand away. 'Excuse me, Mister, ha!' Her laugh choked her, and she was struggling to breathe.

'Oh, it's not so special,' he said as he pushed back her sweaty hair from her face. 'My question is, can you take more? As now I feel the need to call the paramedics for you.'

For fucks sake, does he read my thoughts? The idea made her pussy throb harder, and her thighs opened again, she wanted to feel him more.

'I know you want it; I just want you to show me how much and how hard you do.' His finger was tracing soft lines up her legs, circling her thighs and rubbing he slit through her wet panties.

No thoughts about anything further than this – she wanted him but couldn't voice it, and with a snap of his fingers, he turned from her and walked away.

You don't own me, she angrily thought, fuck you – and I don't think I will.

She straightened herself and lent back in the bar. 'You wanna set me a few of the drinks I was promised?' she said to the bartender while reaching for his hand.

'Sure, but you're his whore, and I'm not going there,' he replied.

Her eyes flashed furiously, and that anger, that had been a concern of her doctor reared up again. 'He doesn't fucking own me! Or who's cock I suck; you wouldn't turn down my wet pussy you limp shit! Oh, and by the way, what gives you the right to call me a whore you prick? I'll take that drink. '

'Sorry I can't, no, just no,' and he pushed her hand away.

She laughed and got up to leave as the dark-haired kitten appeared, tapping her ass. Her soft touch made Crystal quiver.

Fucking lesbian, the voice whispered, as she began to cum under the girl's stoke.

'That's what I wanted.' She gasped as her pussy succumbed the girl touch.

'Oh I know, honey pie,' the girl replied. 'And I think you made a little conquest with your dramatics. Just I been watching for the nod from a certain someone and just got it. Makes my day when I please him, and the rewards will not be shared with you… just yet. We've got to test your capacity. Do you want to be a bird in the cage for a little while? I have some pretties for you to put on that will suit you just fine.'

Crystal didn't want her to stop touching but also wanted to please her. 'Oh wow, I'd love that,' she groaned as the girl flicked her wet bean through her panties.

'Come with me then, no pun intended.'

She took Crystal's fingertips sensuously and guided her through the club to a dark door, hardly visible and opened it with a fob attached to her collar.

'C'mon then sweets,' she softly said. 'You wanna be a Kitten I think, and I'm all for charity. Wanna make you the most desirable creature you can be. You see, our Daddy likes to be spoiled but also for them that are chosen to enjoy the trip. I think I have just the perfect accessory for you and our very special cage.'

Crystal followed her in; she was utterly bewitched at what lay before her as it filled her eye and soul until she felt she would burst.

Costumes and feathers, makeup and lights. Girls, Kittens were naked or partly dressed tending to each other, nuzzling, and kissing and empowering each other for their time entertaining the club's clients. Crystal noticed two, one sitting on the other on a chair, kissing profoundly and so gently. The senior kitten took the others hand and pushed between their naked bodies to her pussy and groaned, biting her lip as the girl found her target. She found herself staring, wanting her pussy to be at that young kitten's mercy and knew she'd never been in a place like this but felt like it fitted,

Except I'm top cat now girls, I sees ya eyeing me, wanting to know me secrets, well I've news for ya, I ain't got no secrets, and that's me pull. I don't try to hook the fish they just fucking jump at me.

She waited for the voice to bark at her, it didn't, but she knew it was waiting, biding its time in its creepy shadow in her mind.

Her attention was pulled back into the room by another Kitten's comment,

'Baby girl,' she said to a small curvaceous blonde. 'No one comes back from the cage, so consider yourself lucky.'

An ebony beauty replied, 'Hell yeah and you know what else? I say he prefers us to them that goes in coz for fucks sake they just disappear. There's something in it. He doesn't wanna lose his main attractions to his private kink. No, them little birds are dispensable'. She waved her beautiful slender arms about, and the rest of the girls ate up her speech hungrily.

Crystal smiled to herself. *WOW, I went straight to the top, no going back if I do well in MY birdcage.*

'Oh hey,' Crystal's girl shouted. 'Are you trying to scare my little bird of paradise? Coz if you are, then there's always a few fat fucks who need their cocks sucking, quite sure I have a few ripe ones who like to keep the week-old scent on them? Do you want to play with me girls? I can have you eating cheese for breakfast, lunch and dinner if you don't quit it…'

The girls giggled and eyed Crystal, but their smiles melted as her mentor stared straight back at them, showing her displeasure openly.

'Oh, a natural, so sweet,' one said.

'But that will never do,' another replied.

'And so that's why I have her here! Now, when you ladies have finished gassing, you can leave me to it. You know this process is secret and kind of sanctified, so go on now and get!' The dark-haired beauty announced with authority.

They bustled past, and the ebony beauty stopped in front of Crystal. 'A kiss for you, precious.' She slipped her wet tongue inside her mouth, her full lips soft as she ventured around every hot part.

Crystal groaned as the girl pushed her back and left laughing with the others.

'I'm Sadie, so as you know what to call me if it gets too much,' the dark receptionist said.

'Sadie, that suits you,' Crystal replied nervously.

The Kittens on the chair were still heavily involved and petting deliciously, with no interest in what was happening outside their world. Sadie took no notice of them either but stared directly at the others still in the dressing room. In contrast, Crystal was having trouble watching the chair Kittens enjoy each other with such emotional love.

That's the sort of love only two girls can feel, she thought.

But then I'm forgetting Mister…, no ours will, is fiercer, and already he treats me like his queen!

The other Kittens quickly finished dressing and followed the others onto the club floor.

The dressing room was burgeoning with beautiful sparkles and costumes, strangely her fingers traced the brim of a top hat and slid down to the rest of it, Not much glitter but pure class and gold.

`I always say that a girl that's to perform her most important dance should also be allowed to choose her colours.' Sadie took the costume from the rail,.'I'd say this is a perfect fit for you. Go on then try it, don't be shy. I've seen everything I need to already.'

Crystal blushed with well-practised bashfulness taking it from her. She slipped out of her clothes, holding the costume to her in front of the large brightly lit mirror.

'I can still see your ass, you know, sweets!' Sadie slapped it and sat down on a stool to the side. 'Go on baby, try it.'

Crystal put the top hat on giggling, 'I like this!' She turned around to face Sadie dressed only in her top hat; her fair skin reflected around the mirrors and nipples ruby red under the lights, her arousal evident. Body unblemished and slim, her thighs showing off her pussy and framing her labia beautifully. 'I feel so special.'

'So, you should see my little bird of paradise, you were singled out. Now I'm gonna leave you to dress, and I'll be back in five to take you to the special cage, ok little one? Oh, and don't forget to apply some oil to that beautiful skin of yours.'

She turned and closed the door softly behind her. Crystal squealed, *Hey you voice, demon. Look at me now! And with none of your help!*

That's just fucking precious ain't it, you're sure? Are you sure I had nothing to do with this?

But she was lost in a sea of rhinestone, thong and black silk so didn't heed the warning… the voice could be so evil, to any others so transparent, as for those it infected there was a blurring of their perception as it's evil nature to an innocent, was irresistible.

All dressed up, she turned to face herself in the mirror and snatched up some makeup.

Yeah, the lights don't much favour the natural look, fucks sake girl put some fakery on!

'Oh, shut up you pathetic figment of my imagination,' she replied. 'I was gonna anyway!' but it hurt her. 'Hey you, you don't belong here. Go back to sleep, Tuppence, I left you behind years ago you weak fuck.'

She buried the memories away along with a conscience that she detested and continued applying fake lashes, lippy and glitter.

The Kittens on the chair took no notice of Crystal's mumblings, one now kneeling on the floor with her head buried in the others crotch, her legs pushed wide and high in the air and her fingers wrapped in the other's hair, clamping her face to her pussy.

The door opened, and Sadie gasped. 'Oh my you're such a special one! I do believe a bonus is coming my way with this acquisition. Darlin' listen to me, I'm a good person, but not everything in life is as it seems or appears to be. I know what you want, and I'll deliver it to you. If

I said to you that you were suicidal, would you deny it? I know you're desperate baby, I know, and I wanna hug you now, come to me baby, come and fill me up.'

Crystal ran to her and flung her arms about her neck, 'Thank you Sadie and you are right. Up until now, I had no thought of living, and I wanted to die. Now I feel so special. These fine clothes, they make my heart pound and that I'm to dance in the prettiest cage, oh wow you couldn't have been kinder to me. Why? Why when I'm not so special?'

Sadie blushed and buried her chin in Crystal's shoulder. 'Girl it's that which makes you unique. Now for the cream, kitty kitty.'

She went to the far side of the dressing room and ran her finger along all the pretty black collars that hung there. 'Mm-hmm, this one.' She slid it off its hook and softly waved it in front of Crystal. 'Daddy's Kitten gotta have a collar and Daddy's Kitten gotta have his mark.'

She slipped a small black disc inside a transparent bell on the collar. It had an X on it, and Crystal licked her dry lips with anticipation, grabbing a glass of neat vodka from the side and letting it slide down her throat, warm and relaxing. Sadie laughed as she softly brushed her hair from her neck and slipped the collar around her dainty throat.

'There now you're all ready, and here,' she filled her glass again, and one for her. 'A toast to the dark road. May it be all you fantasised about and deliver that which you secretly dreamed of.' They raised their glasses and slammed down the drink together.

'Now listen carefully to the Kitten rules.' Sadie lifted her chin to face her. 'Clients are number one. What they want is what the club and the Kittens ensure they get. Do you understand?'

Sadie carried on as Crystal nodded. 'As soon as you arrive in the club you will put your collar on, this collar is now yours as long as you are with us, however short or long that may be, of course. Your collar is not, and I repeat for you, my dear, is not allowed to leave the club ever! Remember that it is crucial. Once you have a client's token, you are theirs and theirs alone, do not fool around or accept any other clients token, dance for all but remember who you belong to. Unless of course, your client wants to share you or watch you with someone else.'

Sadie winked and licked her lips,

'And the last rule, to look after our Kittens, if a client steps over accepted behaviour within the club, we will deal with it straight away. Never hit a client in the club; you may scratch or bite a client if they ask you to, of course, but leave the aggression to the sexy security.' Crystal nodded, and it all made sense.

Sadie grabbed her hand, called out the kittens still on the chair to hurry up out onto the floor and pulled Crystal into the pulsing vibe of the club. 'Now you just do what comes naturally. I know you wanna ask me, but that certain gentleman likes you for what you are. If that means you look like an idiot in that cage, then so be it, just be you.'

She touched Crystal's little nose and softly took her

to the floor until the beautiful cage beckoned her to enter.

'Up to you now, baby, and don't disappoint me.'

She left her clinging on to the cage door, her heart bouncing and the music and scene before her making her want to perform and be a part of.

CHAPTER 4

CRYSTAL TREMBLED AS SHE SCANNED THE HEAVING CLUB.

She felt rooted to the spot, and her mouth became so dry she started to cough. The voice was rasping as it whispered in her ear and hurt her feelings.

Times when it spoke like this it was like a knife scratching her eardrum, and she winced at the pain and the words.

Stupid cunt, what's your problem?

Fucks sake, you look so ugly with your lips sticking to your teeth and your mouth all puckered. Just get in the cage and let the juices flow!

'Daddy,' she sighed, remembering his words to her and her haughty reply.

My Juices? Ugh, you pervy little freak you have gone and embarrassed yourself there.

She giggled hysterically catching a sob in her throat as the voice continued.

He's dead and rotting, you fucking sado.

She laughed again though this time it was whimsical,

remembering her father's face and voice. Churning up her nervous energy, she grabbed the cage door swinging her legs around and moving sensuously down the bars. The music pumped around her body, and as she began to draw more attention, she wanted it fiercer and hotter as other dancers shadowed her in their cages.

The clients of The Collared Kitten, who fumbled in dark recesses and fucked wildly any way they wanted, lapped up her moves voraciously and the scene became an orgy of unspoken lusts.

Crystal wished she could see in the booths. Why had some closed the curtains? For full privacy?

What the fuck are you up to, you need to hide it in here?

She felt a tap on her ass and let a bony manicured finger slip in her lips and stroke her pussy possessively. All that raw rage welled up again as she whipped around ferociously to see who dared fuck with her moves. 'Fucking ruined it!' she screamed as she flashed her eyes at the female client who was eyeing her up lustfully.

She was elegant in a gaunt way with grey hair parted neatly on the left side and a contrived wave tucking under her chin. She had a man's tuxedo on with spiky high heels and silver rings on each thumb and finished her stern look with a slither of red lipstick. Crystal loved how she assessed people so precisely and within seconds of seeing them. 'Fucking dyke,' she smirked, hoping the voice had enjoyed her summation.

Sociopathic freak, the voice replied. *You wanna cut her, don't you? Tut tut, you'll end up back behind bars just not these pretty ones. You better suck ass, you fucking psycho.*

Crystal was still clenching her fists, the severe-looking woman wagged her finger.

'Oh you're new, baby. A little word to the wise, you don't talk to anyone here in that tone, but hey I'll let it slide as you're so gorgeous and I don't want an angry kitty.' She traced a finger down the curve of Crystal's neck, circling her soft nipples and bringing them to arousal. It made her feel sick as dismissively she pushed the woman's finger away.

She knew she had to apologise if she was going to stand any chance here, but she wanted to hurt her just a little bit, she had to drink something as her mouth was so dry the rage was still burning in her.

Otherwise, she would have replied with a hurtful retort.

She spat in her hand, covering her mouth as if she was shyly laughing. A look of horror came across the lesbian clients face.

'Ugh, I see an X! Oh hey, how was I supposed to know? You're just another new face, and there's a tonne here tonight. Well, usually Sadie is around to divert people from chosen ones. Where is that damned girl?'

She stepped back, visibly shaken as Sadie came up to her. 'If you come with me, I'm sure I have something more suitable for you, no need to bother our angry little kitten she has fierce claws and teeth you know?'

The client cleared her throat. 'If you could explain that to him. I'm just so vain and decided to leave my glasses at home, and the X didn't become clear until I had touched her, and you see...'

'Oh honey, there's no need to appear attractive to

any of our Kittens; it's for them to appear so to you and as for the other clientele, I'm pretty sure you could streak with a dildo up your ass, and they'd still not notice you, ha-ha! Honestly, sweets, I prefer you with glasses, hmm? Adds a certain something, let's call it distinction. Showcases your vintage and for sure there's none as vintage as you here, and still so hot and juicy, wow! That's some dedication you have there and must cost a fortune in products.'

Sadie's face was the picture of sweetness yet was a vicious barbed attack a warning. Still, it saved the client who knew, only too well that she had been humiliated to prevent any repercussions and was perversely grateful.

'You're a good girl, Sadie I sometimes wish that you...'

'Oh, no lady, Daddy would never have that. I'm not for sale at any price and to be honest, there's nothing left to purchase if you catch my drift? She took her hand and led her away from an incredibly frustrated and angry Crystal.

That's it, fuck off you ugly old biddy. Ugh god, how the fuck do I make a first impression again?

Her brain itched, and a snarl etched its way across her usually soft lips, she bit hard as the voice replied bringing a little comfort in its own harsh way,

All eyes are on you, you fucking idiot! You're his, and that was perfect, fucking ace! I reckon they never saw anything like it.

It laughed hysterically, and a sly smile crept around her lips as she grabbed the cage again, but this time she would be unmolested. Her oiled body slid down the bars as she stretched out her legs and stepped inside, whipping her hair and beating her body against the cage like the animal, she knew she was - wild and dangerous and now thoroughly aroused, the rage always did that to her.

A tiny perch inside was perfect for exploiting her assets as her body tried to maintain balance, pumping to the sexual sounds of Madonna's Erotica. She worked her body hard to her beat, a song she knew well so was in time and no awkward pauses and felt a fake for fooling the clients,

I fucking practised it a million times in my room you stupid cunts. Hey voice, why does that make me feel like shit?

She knew it would enjoy her state but also knew it wouldn't let it end there.

Because you stupid fuck, you wanna be natural, but you're a fake for as long as you hide. Well, I certainly don't need to mention the name now.

It slithered away from its laughter, becoming one with the music. The horror that filled her made her brave, and the hustler in her beat its way to the forefront of her mind. Her body relaxed, and her confidence returned. She checked herself in one of the mirrors.

Fierce Bitch.

She began to move like the pro she had fantasised she was and, unsure if she would only get one song in the cage, she savoured every beat.

Madonna's sexual sounds were perfect, and she moved around the cage playing with her body, squeezing her breasts through her costume. Her hands teased the audience, playing with her groin through the material. Furtively she looked around, all eyes were on her, and the other dancers were left to kick their feet angrily and gossip with each other with gestures.

Some mocked her by mimicking, but she loved it and ate it up, tasting their blood. She loved cutting people; however, she chose to do it.

No clients came close, but all watched with admiration,

He'll be watching, she whispered to the voice. He will love this, love me, his first choice. Look at 'em, all gagging for a bit of me, yet none can touch except him.

Catalyst, the voice replied proudly.

How do you mean? She replied, her body still aching and pussy throbbing passionately, she had never felt so driven or hungry for someone.

You're your own catalyst, you just make this so enjoyable for me.

She giggled, not really understanding the music was ending, as was her time in the cage. Sadie appeared, smiling and giving her the 'perfect' sign.

Crystal scowled angrily to herself.

You made me fucking miss it, what I was doing? I wanted to feel their eyes on me more. It gets me fucking hot, ok. Now fuck off you bore; I have new friends and a new significant person in my life. I aren't lonely anymore.

As Sadie came closer and held open the cage door, Crystal wiped the sour look from her face and replaced it with an angelic smile.

'Come now honey, oh my that was so impressive!' Sadie proudly remarked,

`C'mon now sweets, time to leave,' she said more forcefully as Crystal began to move again and ignored

Sadie's outstretched hand. 'Let's not make this embarrassing, baby! You had your time to exhibit, and that happens once, only once in a lifetime, and I have news for you, you just got signed! Mmm hmm, you like? Does that make you purr?' she said as she yanked her out of the cage as sweetly and discreetly as she could.

Crystal caught her breath. 'He liked me?'

'Oh, hell yeah, honey he already liked you, you were kinda on probation. I must say I ain't seen him that happy, I was gonna say in a long time but no, I ain't ever seen him that happy.'

Crystal took her hand and excitedly chatted to her as they moved back to the bar. Although Sadie was attentive, she was also bored, 'Go on now, go enjoy the rest of the night but no touching, ok? And your collar? You can hang that proudly up in the dressing room before you leave.' She pinched her nose, saying, 'It will always be there baby, just protocol you know, it's yours, and you are his, so don't fret.'

Crystal went to kiss her cheek which was met with a firm but gentle push back.

'Honey, do you suffer from dementia? I just told you none of that, now shoo. I'll be watching.'

She disappeared into the crowds and Crystal was left wondering what a girl like her really did in a club if she couldn't prostitute herself for drinks or for admission to a party?

Fucks sake, I can't even dance coz that's just too sexy, and I don't wanna annoy Mister.

She went to the bar reckoning drinks would be on the house. Punters went out of their way so as not to even graze her skin, even when she tried to brush past some. It irritated her until she realised it was just him being possessive and she blushed. She'd never felt so special, not even with her own father.

'Line em up,' she said coldly and confidently to the bartender, who did so expertly but also remind her that she was neither to pull or to get too drunk.

There was a limit on how much he could offer her.

'So, what fucking happens now?' she said, slamming a cocktail down her throat.

'He'll find you,' the bartender replied, unable to meet her eyes. 'I'd suggest some air and, well ,you won't get far before he comes for you. Just you seem so eager for it.' He shared a private joke with another tender which annoyed her, she pushed the glasses one by one off the bar and onto the floor. 'Well I guess I'll take that air then. Ugh, oh damn it. I've gone and made a mess of your nice floor. Be seeing ya!'

A wave of cold regret went through her body as the office curtain twitched.

Fuck, why does ... she did not know if 'it' was male or female, which made it creepier, made her blood run cold.

'Oh, look it's made a fucking mess,' The Bar Tom Cats were straight round to it and cleared it away efficiently with not a word to her, just a general bitchy air that left her feeling defeated.

These types, clubber elite, could put down anyone with tongues like fucking vipers.

She was a little woozy, but nowhere near as drunk as she was used to getting. As she was about to leave, she remembered the collar, softy touching it and stroking it. She skipped through the crowds and into the dressing room. It was eerily quiet and empty as she made her way to where the collars hung. Her dexterous fingers quickly undid it, and she placed it on the hook marked with an X, she wrapped her arms around her body and twirled around hugging herself,

And you're a rich one! Not that I care, or maybe I do a little bit, but that's only because poor people are such bores! Ha, oh wow so what will happen now? Oops, I reckon this place is wired for sound, but hey, I'm drunk, and you chose me for who I am. Mister, that makes me feel so special. I'm going to leave, as seems to be what I'm supposed to do but just one thing, you probably know this, but I like the fight. I don't wanna be, in fact, you didn't choose me for my compliance, did you?'

She giggled as she left the room and quickly made her way through the club, unaware of any others and brimming over with importance and funny confidence which confused her as it felt fake. 'I am fucking totally worthy!' she shouted as she left The Collared Kitten, the cold taking her breath away and revellers replying, 'Go home you're drunk.'

All was in good spirits and comforted her nagging doubts as to whether she would ever see him again or if they'd let her back in tomorrow night.

'Maybe they're fucking laughing at me!' She sobbed a little and decided to walk a while and try to put it down too much drink and maybe a Mickey.

CHAPTER 5

THE WINTER AIR WAS SHARP IN HER THROAT AND LUNGS, and although she had nowhere to stay, she didn't care.

I'd rather sleep in the gutter you cunt, she thought as she turned from the club onto the street.

A long silver limo pulled up beside her as she walked and she knew it was him, she kept walking determined not to be played.

The window lowered, and Robert Alexander poked his head out, 'You're not staying for the final shows then?'

She ignored him, carrying on as best she could. Still, a secret smile played around her lips and her curiosity about what he'd be like betrayed her.

'It's just that I had such plans for you, and here you are not even talking to me.' His softness was enticing, his boldness was erotic, and his wealth was the deal-breaker. She stopped and bent low to meet his eyes in the car, 'Oh Mister, you want me? You don't humiliate me in front of a crowd that could pay my way for a week, no you beg me, Mister, you fucking beg me.'

'Oh, I see,' his voice cold and uncaring made Crystal realise he would not easily be played either. 'Well, I am afraid I do not beg for anything, from no one, especially a pretentious, silly little girl. Serenade and bon voyage.' He turned from her sinking back into the plush leather seats, the window closed smoothly until she could only see her reflection and the car pulled off quickly.

Stunned, she laughed her throaty laugh, 'Fuck you dickhead!' she shouted and began to walk, her heels in her hand, the cobbled floor cool on her sore feet and she enjoyed that more than anything else she had all night. She sat on the curb and stretched out her skinny legs, silently watching those that passed and allowing the dawn to warm her shoulders as it began to appear. She was massaging her feet as the limo pulled up again, 'Want a lift?' he said, staring her right in the eye and with as much confidence as was needed.

'Nah, you ok – I quite like it here.' she replied but laughed bitterly at how she felt obsessed with him already, she wanted to control this but didn't want to risk losing this meal ticket.

'You're sure? Only I see a little girl with nowhere to go who wants a taste of me like it's setting her on fire. Not to mention my wealth, oh yes you did that already didn't you, or was that just what you were thinking?' He opened the car door, stretching his lower body out she could see, his hard cock in his hand, angry, so thick it made her pussy pulse. *Impressive!* She thought, wondering how it would feel in her throat as it began to cum.

Her tongue pushed hard against the roof of her mouth to suppress the tantalising sensation building.

Her body reacted to the lust she sensed and felt overwhelming arousal, her heart thumped quickly. She'd never hooked one so exceptional in all her days.

'I could use a lift,' she said, staggering forward, wanting desperately to feel him.

'Get in,' he said forcefully, as she crawled into the back leaning towards him and feeling his hot mouth penetrate hers. He pulled her onto his lap, his hands pushed her pelvis and her pussy onto his cock as his tongue searched out parts of her mouth that she had never felt tongued before. His cock was hard against her wet panties, she wanted to peel the damp material aside and let him slide in her, but she wanted him to want it more.

He was not going to beg her she realised that, but she needed to see the lust he had for her in his eyes.

The car slowly pulled away; windows blacked out. It slowly made its way through Soho and the short distance to Mister Robert Alexander's penthouse.

She was naked within seconds, her bra keeping her wrists bound and her knickers around her ankles. His hard, bulbous cock was hot against her thigh as he pushed her face down into the limo's warm leather seat. His beautiful manicured nails traced lines down her back, along her bum cleavage, she squealed as they dug in, enjoying the sensation. She wriggled to feel them more. Still, he took them away.

'Don't fucking do that. Fuck my flesh deeply,' she groaned as his fingers became soft and stroked her back softly. 'I don't wanna be a boring work of art. I wanna be your fucked-up Picasso,' she growled, trying to make him hurt her again.

He reached down, taking a handful of her hair and brought her back up, so his mouth was beside her ear. She could feel his breath on her and struggled to not show how hot it made her, how her nipples reacted to him, not wanting to give away how hooked she was. He was like a hot fucking drug she could not get enough of. She panicked as she felt his hands on her neck, but his skin was replaced by a leather collar, it was the collar from the club.

Crystal knew this was against The Collared Kitten rules. Sadie had gone over and freakin' over them with her. She began to protest, thinking, *This fuck has blown the job for me.*

He gripped her neck tightly, and she froze. Firmly, he told her, 'Whenever you are with me you will wear your collar and know you are my kitten to pleasure and do whatever I want with. No one in the club will question this, and you are not to discuss this with anyone. Do you understand?'

She felt the power within his fingertips around her throat as she forced a nod of confirmation. She found his total domination of her such an overwhelming turn on, hearing herself gasp as he eased his grip. She usually dominated in a sexual liaison knowing she had to control this man to her advantage, but fucking how? When all she wanted was for him to crush her and show her how high she could get on him. He turned and pushed her down, so her back was on the leather.

he felt his head go between her hot throbbing thighs, and his tongue softly take her clit and massage it until she was screaming and crying in ecstasy. She wanted his cock or fingers inside her deeply pushing and spreading her wider. She pulled her pussy away from his lips and tongue, begging him to stop. Roughly he grabbed her beautiful mane and pushed her head down to his masterful, wonderful cock, his hands on her back groaning as her tongue started to circle his tip and lips played with is foreskin. She slowly, deliberately, took him deep into her mouth.

His grip was wound tightly around her hair, pulling her deeper onto his choking, ridged, wet, cock, she needed to breathe, but he held her tightly on it. As her eyes rolled back and her hands desperately pushed herself away, he eased her head off him, smiling as she coughed and sputtered, thick reams of spit and pre-cum hanging from his cock to her mouth.

She flashed an angry glare at him, which faded quickly as she felt so wanton, fucking hoe and turned on by his aggression, No one ever dared that with her before. She knew he needed to feel her deep. He pulled her from the footwell up onto the seat and slid two fingers into her wetness. Her legs naturally lifted and parted to give him total access to her juicy pulsing cunt.

'Ugh yeah!' she gasped. 'Oh Mister, please, I want it bad!'

He pushed her thighs apart more, making her feel like a wishbone being pulled apart and buried his face further into her. Her cries made his attack feverish and his cock so hard that she knew he would want to fuck her soon. Still, he was enjoying the wait, playing with her needs and his patience too much, watching her desperation to feel him deep inside.

'Whatever the fuck you are just please god fuck me! I've never been so hot.'

He raised himself from her exposed and sodden pussy, leaning forward over her. 'Slut,' he whispered in her ear, as he started finger-fucking her with four fingers, spreading her even more. He rose up so she could feel his hard-on pressed against her wet cunt. Crystal's head rolled back while she pushed her pussy onto his cock, 'Fuck me, you bastard, just fuck me.'

He drove in his cock's head and circled it, her juices smothering him he let out a deep moan that made her ears and throat cum, she was still so tight and soft, and his cock needed in her. Her eyes popped as he grabbed her throat, digging his thumb into her windpipe as he pushed his cock in her deeply and with total selfish abandonment, all the way in.

She screamed as his hot hard on stretched and burned slightly as her cunt became used to the size filling her deeply. She loved it, needed it; she'd never felt that hot or full before. It felt on fire... fucking amazing, she thought, feeling close to passing out but orgasming hard. Her pussy and body demanded more pleasure from his magnificent manhood.

Rocking slowly, his fingers tight around her throat, she tried to press harder against him which he rewarded with a sharp spank on her thigh, she loved it and kept pushing, to feel him chastise her more.

His thrusts became quicker and harder. She felt him

about to ejaculate and was crying out of fear as his grip on her throat became fierce. But she wanted more, her body was feeling light and full, her nipples so sensitive wanting more. It was intoxicating. she'd never felt scared while fucking before, he grabbed her hips, while she gasped for the new air and rode her hard.

'Whore, you're fucking beautiful,' he let out. It annoyed him, and he spanked her harder.

She loved this submission and rewarded it. 'Ugh, god you cunt,' she cried as he capitulated inside her. She wriggled, feeling the hot spurt. Her muscles gripped him tighter as his cum filled her. He kept pumping her hard, not willing to stop just because he had cum once. That was nothing compared to what this beast could do, and she knew it. His cock stayed hard, and she was panicking that his grip was getting tighter around her throat, her breath now rasped, but god she needed everything he could give.

He turned her over onto all fours without breaking that hot wet liaison between his cock and her pussy, pushing her head down on to the leather. Crystal found the smell intoxicating. She was used to fabric or plastic car seats which normally smelt of stale sweat or sickly-sweet polish. He continued to slide his cock into her wetness, his hand moved from her throat and grabbed her hair which he used to push her face firmly against the soft leather of the seat again.

'You're such a dirty bastard,' she yelled out.

He pulled her back by her hair. 'That's Daddy, to you from now on,' which filled her with butterflies in the pit of her stomach.

She'd heard him called it by chosen ones in The Collared Kitten but never dreamed he'd be her Daddy. He cracked her ass so hard that she fell forward. As she landed back on the seat, he drove himself deep into her, enjoying her body bounce on the leather and pushing her deeper onto him. His hand pulled his belt from his trousers, she heard the leather flick through each loop of the belt in fast succession, part of her wanting to run but the part ruling her choices decided that she wanted to feel it.

She looked back and saw him grip the buckle and wrap the leather tightly around his hand, the broad, thick hide creaking as he pulled it tight until enough of the belt hung down, like the shape of a flaccid penis.

Crystal's body tensed at what she was expecting, tightening around his cock, she feared that he would be cruel and too much, but surely, he was going to tease her, play her? She felt herself gulp in fear and began riding his cock, hoping this may make him continue fucking instead. She was cumming at the thought of feeling the leather across her ass cheeks.

He allowed the belt to hang close to her face, he wanted her to see the beauty of the belt, and of course, he wanted her to know this was thick and well stitched not a flimsy piece of leather, and she was going to feel it.

He slid out of her, she was so angry, his teasing unbearable but increasing her lust to feel him cum in her again. She knew now that there was no escaping the sting of his belt as it disappeared, and she braced herself in anticipation.

There was nothing, she held a breath deep and

panicked but stayed still and braced, still nothing. It was just seconds, but her mind was going crazy.

What's going on? Why has he not hit?

She turned to look back and suddenly felt the flick of leather against her skin, the sound assaulting her ears. She let out a scream, followed by a deep turned on growl. God, she liked it, liked it a lot. She jumped in shock and immediately felt betrayed by her body as if revealing some major secret. He had only grazed her hot ass with it. He reached down, placing his hand around her throat again and bringing her ear to his lips.

He kissed it and whispered, 'Just a little pain, a little encouragement to please Daddy.' He flicked her cheek with an upward stroke which she loved.

'Hurt me,' she cried, wanting more depravity. He smiled and pushed her back down onto all fours. 'Hurt me, Daddy?' he said, flicking harder this time, 'Remember your manners girl and who I am to you!'

She winced from the leather. 'Ugh yeah Daddy, hurt me more., she sobbed, but the pleasure made her lose control.

She was pressed against the seat as he began to punish her, each stroke of the belt making her cum repeatedly until she felt like she was dying. Each crack through the air was followed with a thwack across her rear. Her screams were increasing in volume, but after the first five strikes, the sounds merged into one orgasmic mixture of pleasure and pain.

She wanted more but did not know if she could take it, where were those fingers, could he fuck her ass now as she was prostrated with her ass exposed and pussy dripping

Crystal had lost count, and her buttocks felt like he had made them bleed. Daddy was obviously not new to this type of pleasuring, and she dismissed any fear but broke on the next lash.

'No, Daddy, no more please, it hurts. Ugh but I like it? No just stop, it's too much,' she cried tears running from her cheeks as her pussy and ass throbbed with desire and heat.

She was so confused but knew he was loving that, watching her reactions like a predator. She needed more of him inside her, needed to feel his all, have all her holes filled and stretched.

Robert Alexander was not interested in Crystal's pleading, enjoying her guttural squeals and trembling against his hard body.

The lines across her ass were vivid red as it trembled but still, she wanted, needed more, though knew she really couldn't take it. He lent back, still hard and stroking his cock, she turned to face him, and naturally, her eyes lowered when he met hers. Where she was used to talking and thinking for herself, she had no thought but to watch him, if he allowed.

He raised her chin with his soft fingers so she could see him wanking slowly. 'I wanna touch, Mister, let me please?' She begged, her pussy so aroused that she began to touch herself, wanting to please him.

'I'm the sweetest you ever had, Mister,' she thought as she watched his beautiful hard on jerking and wet.

His hand struck her, already sore butt harshly,

sending pain shooting through her body. 'That's what you will feel when I have to remind you, girl, to you I am Daddy!'

He lifted her chin again, smiled and wiped the tears from her eyes. 'If I want you to think for yourself, I'll tell you to.'

He pulled her head down to his cock and fucked her mouth till his cum, creamy, hot and salty, spewed down her throat, and sides of her lovely mouth, she heard him through gritted teeth which made her feel so fucking hot, so she sucked harder.

'I know what you are thinking, Baby Girl, I know every thought,' he groaned as she sucked and licked until no taste of cum was left. She licked along his hard shaft and took in his balls into her mouth. Licking his stomach and thighs, lovingly consuming all the juice her lips and tongue could find. It was mixed with the sweat from his body which was intoxicatingly addictive, and she couldn't believe that he was still hard.

What is he on? How can he keep it up so long?

A pang of fear shot through her, worried if she had taken on more than she could deal with, but then that faded and beautiful tantalising confidence waded in.

'I'm gonna bleed your wallet you cunt, bleed you and fuck you. You wanna filthy whore? It's gonna cost you!'

He sat back into the seat with his legs wide in the footwell, he pulled her on top of him, facing away from him. She could clearly feel his erection against her buttocks and knew how he planned pleasure, feeling her strong anus muscle clench instinctively. Not that she had never indulged in anal sex. Ugh god no, like, that's something I only do in long term relationship not just wild fucking!

Was it curiosity that stopped her saying no? Or just pure animal lust? It scared her knowing she would happily fuck his cock with her arse, but was confused as to her immediate compliance.

Maybe this is it, yeah this is who, what I've been waiting for.

Where would her limits be with him? It was clear that as soon as she said no, she would be out, that had always been her way, but now it turned her off, and she cried out, 'Fuck it!' With all his power and sexual prowess, she knew he was no rapist. The people in The Collared Kitten all gave their respect to him, staff and clients alike.

She knew she would provide him with everything and risk everything.

Hell yeah, the money is cool and comforts too, but I wanna give this cunt his deepest darkest fantasies and served up on a cheap common whore from the backwaters.

Robert lifted her legs outside his, spreading her thighs and pussy, her vagina leaking a cocktail of his hot thick cum and her musky sex juices.

She glanced up, catching the drivers eyes watching her in the rear-view mirror. She felt ashamed and embarrassed to have caught him watching, and she pushed her thighs as close together as possible, covered her pussy and breasts and turned her face away.

'Do you want to please your Daddy, girl?' He grabbed a handful of her now messy hair and pulled her head back to face the driver's gaze.

'Watch him! I want you to be wanted,' he said, as he reached down and spread her thighs again as far as comfort would allow.

He pulled her hand away from her pussy, and she saw the driver's eyes widen. His cock throbbed against her buttocks, so she placed her hand on the limo roof as he firmly removed her other hand from her tits and placing it around his huge penis. His hand guided hers as he made her draw back his foreskin, slowly covering and exposing his gland in generous, deliberate movements.

She could feel his wetness against her back until he lifted her hand and enclosed it around his large bulbous wet end. She groaned at the feel of his delicious cock, thinking to herself, *He's hooked on me... wanker can't get enough*. She was pleased and disappointed at the same time to be wanking him off, but escaping this huge monster being squeezed into her ass.

His hand released hers that was supporting her on the roof of the vehicle and slid his fingernails along her arm, over her breast, squeezing her erect nipples briefly and scratching down across her stomach to her pussy. He stroked her wet, soft vagina.

'You like him watching?' he whispered as the driver peered in. 'We are going to show him what a dirty little whore you are.'

Crystal wanted to hide, she was proud of her body and happy to show it off dancing, but that was to who she decided to show it to not for others to choose for her. He parted her sex lips wider with his fingers. He rubbed along the wetness inside with his middle finger circling her vagina opening, teasing her then sliding along her slit until he reached her clit. Hardly touching it he smiled at her reaction, she was so turned on by his touch, she wanted to feel his cock slide inside her again and fuck her.

She pushed her legs wider, wanting him to at least finger fuck her. 'Fuck me, please Daddy,' she panted. 'Ugh god, I never needed it so bad. I'll be whatever you want.'

She started arching her back to try and release some of the tension building in her cunt and arse.

'I know,' he answered, continuing to play with her wet slit, knowing how much she wanted him to give her release. He teased her opening, which was dripping in anticipation, sliding in his fingertip. She tried to push her hips forward to feel him deeper, but he was not giving her what she craved. He let go of her hand on his cock, but she held on tightly.

His hand moved around her waist, over her stomach and breasts and gripped her throat, she moaned in pleasure. He pulled her body back towards him and whispered in her ear, 'Daddies whore is going to fuck his cock'

'Oh yes Daddy, I want it so bad, please let me ride your cock my pussy is so wet for you'

'No, you whore, you are going to ride my cock with your arse! Do you understand?'

'But Daddy, my pussy is so wet for you now, you are so bad for me. Pure evil for my pussy, don't you wanna treat your girl?'

His grip tightened around her neck, the shock

making her whelp as he squeezed her throat. 'It's all a treat for you, Baby girl,' he replied, with his well-placed thumb digging in her orgasmic throat. She had another choice to make quickly, and although she had hoped to keep her butt for later, she realised she was already lifting herself and guiding his head up and down her slit, mixing their juices.

Dragging the mixed cream to the back of her slit and finding her tight muscle, spreading the juice all around. Her legs were shaking violently, and she was angry with herself, not used to her body, having so little control. With his glans coated in their cum, she guided him to her ass. Her eyes opened as she glanced in the mirror, seeing the limo driver wanking and staring at her.

She felt ashamed again and just closed her eyes hoping he did not crash, thinking, *please god, don't let my family find me dead with a cock up my arse.* The driver quickly became nothing to her consciousness, as her hot frenzy for her Daddy begged her again to ride his cock and to ride it hard.

She could feel its heat against her ass muscle, still gripping as she pushed herself on it but was scared, wondering if she would be able to force his cock in or if it would hurt too bad as it was the biggest she'd had.

Her mind raced, fear and lust mixed in a potent cocktail, and she had to have his all.

Perverted cunt, she thought as she caught the driver watching again.

Robert Alexander was rubbing her clit slowly and massaging her throat with his other steady hand. 'Come on, girl, Daddy is waiting to feel your inner arse,' he whispered.

She pushed again feeling her ass give a little more, she was so relieved she had covered his head with her natural pussy lube. She pushed hard against his cock and felt his glans opening her up like never, she gasped loudly as now the pleasure she had been feeling was painful. 'Please Daddy, no I can't it's too big, it will tear me …. ahh … please … '

This was followed by a deep groan and tears as Robert used both hands to grip her and slide himself inside of her.

Her ass muscles desperately closed around his length as his cock slid past. He let out a groan that sounded both like pleasure and triumph.

She felt a burst of shocking pain, followed by the feeling that she was going to ass cum. The feeling was wild to her, and she began to slowly ride his cock sensually and erotically, driving herself deeper on this relentless shaft of pleasure.

As she rode, she felt his stiff fingers enter her pussy, spreading his fingers wider, releasing her throat to play with her clit; squeezing it, flicking it and rubbing it. She couldn't look at the driver, she felt humiliated by Robert Alexander but couldn't say no, the sex was just way too fucking good.

It was hotter still by the fact she beat the other girls to this luxury, some must have tried before, but me, the new girl has got him, and he wants it bad.

She had little control over the depth his cock was rammed in her arse. Her feet were off the floor, each time she dropped herself back down onto his raging hard-on, she let out screams of ecstasy as he buried himself deeper each time.

His cock sunk deeper into the inners of her while he continued finger fucking - so fast now, teasing and playing with her clit. She felt like she was gonna pass out but just kept cumming, not able to catch her breath.

Opening her eyes to see the driver about to cum, they feverishly fixated on him and his cock as she watched him ejaculate to her, or was that to him? He is so fucking horny. Robert Alexander's sexual appetite was taking her to heights she had never known, and she had lost count of how many times she'd orgasmed, wanting to feel him release deep inside her.

Now exhausted, she was pleased to feel the growth in his cock, feel his muscles tightening.

At last, he is gonna cum.

He groaned under her continuous ride. 'Fuck me harder,' he demanded, and Crystal complied, although her body had little energy left.

He gripped her thighs and started thrusting up into her, desperate to release his cum deep inside. He shuddered and let out a loud cry as he released all he had into her depths. She screamed as he bit her shoulder hard, pulling her closer and digging himself deeper.

She cried out in pain, but still, he kept cumming, she could feel him deep inside and his fingers making her wider starting to move faster and faster. She was building to an awful but wonderful climax, making her orgasms so intense.

If I die now, I'm so fucking cool with it.

As things subsided his grip released on Crystal, allowing her to collapse against him. The limo came to an abrupt but smooth stop at which moment Crystal felt a sharp spank on her thigh, 'We are here – sort yourself out girl, this isn't the gutter,' he said flatly.

It was harsh, but she liked it – liked it bad. She slid off his cock - she had to do this slowly as she had been opened so wide.

He still felt firm as she gripped his cock, pulling him out of her, his cum leaking from her now red ass, some dripping onto him and the car and running down her legs. She picked up and pulled on her panties and bra, tidying her long chestnut hair that had some of his juice in.

He smiled as she pulled her panties up giving him a view of her swollen pussy and arse leaking his cum which made her blush girlishly and she hid it as best she could but knew he had enjoyed it.

The driver appeared at the door and ushered them forth he had just watched her most intimate moments jerking himself off to her or him? But she grabbed her dress and covered herself, she had her panties and bra on but was embarrassed as he opened the door for them. The rush of cold fresh air was heady after the sweat and staleness of the sex damned car air, her skin came out in goose bumps and her nipples poked through the bra.

He stood to attention not glancing into the limo interior she slipped into her dress as quick and modestly as she could.

'Devil's Dyke' was the name of the great Georgian manor apartments. Still, it was too much for her to take in and she buried her face in her hair and tried to press closer to him 'Closer to this devil,' she whispered.

As she stepped out of the limo, the driver offered his hand to assist, which made her feel special, and she continued like a little princess. His eyes were glazed and looking straight through them as if he had seen no one exiting the vehicle.

The morning air was fresh and rushed through her nostrils, clearing out that hot, sweaty car air. She could still smell him on her, a strong sensual sandalwood smell, Not surprising.

My panties are soaked and I fucking love that he's still leaking from me.

As Robert Alexander exited the vehicle, he curtly dismissed the driver with a wave of his hand making Crystal feel even more above her own status.

She noticed the driver offer a short bow 'Yes Sir, thank you Sir' in a broad Africans accent as the door was closed, and he swiftly got back into the front of the limo.

She wondered if he would have to clean the vehicle himself and how many people worked for Daddy? She could hear the voice giggling bitterly at her, but tonight was too special to listen.

The only lights on were in reception, he took her hand in a strangely soft and possessive manner leading her to the entrance.

'You like what you see?' He stroked her body, making her spine tingle and body tremble. 'I want you to enjoy the fruits of my, shall we say, labour! I adore secrets, girl, the magic of possession is lost on those that try to achieve it openly as deceit is such a delicious commodity, don't you think?'

His eyes showed a proudness as he emphasised the word 'deceit.'

The elegant cryptic words delighted her, though she didn't understand them fully, answering as well as she could. 'I've never seen a more perfect set up, Mister… Daddy.'

'Good girl, that's how I'd have it – though there are few who would disagree with me, then I'm my own lord and master and answerable to none, do you understand?'

She nodded not out of idiocy but because she knew he'd never be told by another living being.

He opened the door with his fob waving off the ageing receptionist who greeted him, bowing his head slightly, 'Good morning Mr Alexander.'

The receptionist acted like she didn't exist, as if she wasn't there.

'No time for pleasantries with basic sycophants,' he whispered to her mischievously, which she gobbled up, wanting to feel his kind words soothe her where his others had stung. It created a lustful hunger in her for pain and pleasure. His grip on her hand lessened, allowing his fingers to tease her palms and fingertips, guiding her to the lift.

'Tick Tock.' he said, as he keyed the lift to open. 'You're as hot as can be, well for the present it will do. I do like it hot, so much more palatable – I cannot abide cold meat.'

His hand was on the small of her back as he guided

her into the lavish lift. She went to rub up against him again, desperate to feel, smell or hear him – hear the beat of his heart and his steady breath. You trained yourself, didn't you, Mr? To appear all at ease with your posh manners and witty sarcasm, but I see through it. He pushed her back; she caught her breath in her throat. 'I want to wait and savour, taste you when the fire consumes you.'

She sighed huskily.

'Now little girl, Daddy knows best,' as he tucked her hair behind her ear and fondled her sensitive lobe. 'Such soft skin,' he whispered in her ear as the lift ascended to the penthouse. 'Ok little lady,' he pushed her forwards as the doors opened onto his lair.

'Little lady?' she laughed.

'Oh, hush now, you have no idea. You think you're bad, hmm? To me, you're as innocent and untouched as the breaking dawn.'

She blushed uncontrollably, tentatively looking around at the opulent surroundings. The lift doors shut behind them.

A pretty trap, but for who? She thought as a wicked smile ghosted across her face, almost gave her away.

'A delicious last post, rather do you not think?' he said once again freaking her out as though he knew every thought. He pulled her further in and gestured for her to look around.

'We are so similar,' she said with the faintest of whispers, he snapped her back, his nails piercing her wrist flesh, he moved his face directly in front of her, and she noticed a small scar through his eyebrow where before she had to look down like a schoolgirl about to be scolded

'Never assume we are similar sweet girl. You think you're unique? You think that the whole world apart from you is homogeneous?'

She was red-faced and unsure how to take his words, he used them as sexual enticements she was enjoying every syllable.

'Forgive me, I forget that to every girl who ever had a father, they for sure are his princess at some point and perhaps in low times those thoughts warm. So, no you are not a pathetic wretch, and thank goodness for that because I have a bullish habit, of breaking things and, through necessity, have had no option but to come to enjoy it.'

He was laughing and eyeing her reactions, and she lapped up every bit of it but then shuddered as she dismissed thoughts of her own dear departed father.

I'm sorry, Dad, but this is no time to be thinking as your little girl or princess.

CHAPTER 6

'When your eyes have finished doing that silly rolling thing they are doing, perhaps you would like to sit?'

He tickled the inside of her thigh, which was still wet, and she staggered forward onto an elegant new buck leather couch sinking into it, so soft and luxurious, she instinctively closed her legs, 'I know some things, Mr.'

'Really? You surprise me,' he said, interrupting her. 'Forgive me, but I wanted to save us both some blushes.'

She ignored him; his sarcasm was lost on her – at least while she was still quite drunk. 'Excuse me, but my wetness might stain your ever so fine seats here, and I wasn't dragged up.'

As she said the words and saw his reaction, she wished she hadn't spoken.

Idiot – you idiot! You're on your own, the voice snarled, and she sobbed, *Well, I don't like to embarrass myself at least not often, not like tonight, I seem to be all over the place.*

'I don't like to embarrass myself very often, Mister.'

'You must remember it's Daddy. Please refrain from calling me Mister; I'm not a John and you most certainly are not a hooker.'

The last part of his sentence made her heart flutter, she listened for the brutality of the voice to stop her from making a fool of herself, but no thoughts, and it shook her. Relaxing just a little, she scanned the room, which was decorated in a minimalist fashion, some tribal, ancient art scattered about.

Still, everything else was clean, immaculate like it's the owner. Daddy's voice shocks her from her inner voices.

'Drink? Let me guess, vodka, with a dash of our Lady's virginity? You have consumed quite a lot, girl. Bloody Mary?' Not waiting for a response, he fixed it and placed it in her trembling hands, he walked to a table and stroked a delicate decanter. 'Crystal.'

'Huh? I'm sure I never? No, I know I haven't told you my name, so I guess it was Sadie, yeah, that's it, Sadie told you?' She poured the drink down her parched throat, feeling uncomfortable, her heart was racing, and her blood felt like it pumped ice through her veins.

He fingered the beautiful glass again, tracing a line down its length as though a beautiful woman. 'I find people of, shall we say, 'enforced social ineptitude' often bullishly finish other people's sentences with the banalest statements. You see, they have a dependency on aggression that's not always physical, certainly not in your case, Crystal is it? Anyway, they seem to like to shut people down before they make idiots of 'themselves' and then inevitably, Crystal, the aggression follows? Though in your case, I do believe you quite enjoy the pain of humiliation. So, you see,' he picked up the decanter again. 'The finest 17 Century French crystal which has the most delectable glass cuts making the shine and lustre tantalise wanting to be touched. Therefore, you must understand that I was completely oblivious to your name. Quite a strange one to be christened with, though.'

She blushed nervously and pulled her legs up. 'Forgive me – Daddy, is it?'

Knob, she thought, but it sounded different to her.

Still a knob no matter what I believe.

'Here I am thinking I should make myself at home and putting my silly feet up on your expensive furniture.'

He put the decanter carefully back. 'Tut-tut – such insolence, but I have to say it becomes you and the situation one of your standing find themselves in. I do find I am rarely disappointed with an acquisition.'

He beckoned her to him and still giggling she got up and sauntered over as best she could, trying to maintain some sort of allure. Her thoughts were not amusing her as they usually did or filling her with courage through the verbal and psychological battery. She had come to perversely love them but, at this point, couldn't remember when they started or ended.

Before this moment, she had whiled away many hours in full-blown conversation. 'Yes, I'm sure I have had them?' she nervously remarked to herself.

'Oh, those sorts of thoughts are so incredibly dull – you will see.' He pinched her nose. 'Boop! Stop it now,

Baby girl, for Daddy, hmm? Try not to abuse the limited brain cells you possess with questioning things far beyond you.'

She touched his thigh, stroking until she reached his groin feeling his hard muscle, 'Mister, Daddy, I need to feel it again.' Her breath was hot against his throat, he let out a throaty moan,

'Not now, just a while longer little one, you see.' He pointed to the bath. 'Tempted?'

She gazed longing at the beautiful bathing area, marble and ormolu.

'I've never seen or been somewhere so expensive. I'm scared I'll break it all as I'm so clumsy,' she laughed and slipped out of her mini and scant top, skipping over to investigate it with lust and squealed as she pushed a button and the bath began to fill.

She fingered her bra and wet panties girlishly, and oddly, she had never felt so insecure about removing them. His blue eyes travelled up her skinny legs as he walked over to join her. 'Allow me – in such circumstances, I often find my prey a little unwilling.'

He pushed her forward onto the bath and spread her legs, his fingers tore her bra off forcefully as his tongue travelled down her spine to the curve of her rear. Slowly he removed her panties.

'So wet – such a naughty girl.' Turning her to face him, licking down her throat and nipping her nipples, he moved lower between the spread legs his tongue flicked over her clit. His hands pushed her thighs further apart, his masculine form and scent aroused her until she began to feel breathless, he was tonguing her so hard. She cried out loudly as she began to cum again.

'Bathe – 'he said flatly and walked away to sit and watch from an elegant opal coloured leather chair beside the bath. He opened his legs as she tentatively got in the hot foaming bath. He undid his suit trousers releasing his manhood to stand proud and stroked himself as he watched her slowly soap up and begin to relax.

She laid back, sighing, 'Oh Daddy, this is the best I ever felt.'

'Indeed,' his gruff voice was close, and she opened her eyes to see him above her, his hands travelled down her neck pushing her forward. 'Such a mane, but in dire need of washing.'

He pushed her shoulders down until she was submerged. She panicked but stopped as his hand cosseted her neck. 'Fear must be administered slowly to be savoured and trust – I find that incredibly intoxicating.'

He groaned as he felt her relax under the pressure of his hands and pulled her back up massaging her hair, she could feel how wet he was against her as her thighs came up. She rested her knees against the sides of the bath, her hand stroked her full breasts and nipples and drifted down to her pussy.

'I gotta touch, Daddy,' she gasped as her finger slipped in her wetness. 'Ugh, touch me please,' she huskily cried as she stroked herself, wanting him to fuck her – to caress her – to hurt her.'

'A lesson in erotic masturbation of the mind and

body is to always give what's not expected, a little humiliation delivers such delicious results.'

He pushed her forward and walked away. 'Say it then,' he said, over his shoulder.

'You cunt!' she spluttered, closing her legs and grabbing a towel, 'Fuck you, you're... '

'Enough!' he raised his finger, pointing directly at her then circled it as though encircling her. 'I do so enjoy the human spirit but is made even more erotic when accompanied by a depraved amount of wine and food.' He was pulling ingredients from the fridge and laying it on the table, she was out of the bath stood watching him as he laid out olives, cold meats caviar, and salmon. 'Goodness I almost forgot!' he said, fishing in a cupboard, 'No feast of the soul can be complete without a judicious amount of salty, fatty, cheesy potato chips.'

She stood there, trembling. 'I'm dripping. You wanna feel?'

He ignored her, hurrying his chosen dinner. 'If you'd like to eat, you may, but I think I have something you'd rather feast on.' He walked over to her and pushed her to the couch. 'Will you sit, or at least eat?' he growled, fingering her wet hair and neck and perching her on his lap.

She stood up. 'Well, I'm not sure, Mister, ugh, I'm sorry, Daddy. Just I think you need a bit of me more than I need you.'

'Really? You really think that way?' he laughed and flicked her towel away from her wet silky legs. 'Enjoy yourself on your way out,' and pushed her away.

Crystal stood up and went to the lift. 'I'd sooner go home in a towel than stay somewhere I wasn't wanted,' her voice caught in her throat. She waited for what seemed an age for the lift to ping. As it did, he said, 'Oh here you silly girl!'

She blushed, not sure what to do – but she wanted to go to him, felt compelled. Slowly she walked over and sat beside him.

'Let me call you a cab,' he brutally destroyed her fantasy but also made it.

'Oh, my fucking God, you complete knob! But I didn't expect any different!' She stood up, pushing his hands from her hair, 'Fuck you!' she screamed, 'and fuck the neighbours. I'm sure they're more used to your' conquests,' is it? Being more compliant, but then you ain't ever had or likely to have anything like me.' She went to leave, but his hand grabbed hers, stopping her.

He yanked her towards him pushing her down onto him. 'I'll fuck you, thank you very much, Miss. I want your wetness again.' His grip was masterful, he ripped the towel from her body. 'And you were going home in a towel?' he mused as her mouth met his in a hot frenzy.

She went to answer, but his hands on her breasts stopped her, his tongue was in her ear and his cock so hard as she rubbed her wet pussy against it, wanting more of him, wanting him to dominate and hurt her.

His hand slipped around her neck, grabbing her damp hair. 'You filthy little fucking whore,' he whispered in her ear as he pulled her up and carried her to the bed, his hard cock pressed against her wet thighs.

He pushed her face down onto the bed, raising her

rear and tracing his finger across her aching wet hole. 'Don't move,' he said.

She was panting and had no thought to disobey him. She wanted whatever he was going to deliver, so he turned her head to see what he fished for in a drawer. 'And no peeking,' he added as he turned to see her with his hands behind his back. She quickly looked away, stretching her arms out and gripping the pillows.

'For the sake of the neighbours,' he said. 'This could get noisy.' He knelt behind her so she could feel the full length of his hard shaft and slipped a silk gag around her mouth.

She bit on it as he tied it tighter. 'Such a good girl,' he said, stroking her hair and running his hands delicately over her breasts and down her body, she let out a soft sigh as they slipped between her legs and then across her rear. He pulled her back to the edge of the bed and tapped her bottom with something, then waved the crop in front of her eyes, and she braced herself for the sweet agony he was going to give.

Starting gently at first, just brushing her with the end of the crop, sliding it between her bum cheeks, wetting the end just a little by pushing into her wet cunt, biting her in between each stroke. She wanted more – she wanted it harder, his hot breath and teeth grazing her after each whip.

'A little pain to increase the pleasure,' he said as he thrashed her harder. 'And the 'dependency,'' he added, striking her red cheeks until they became sore.

'I'd say for you to tell me when to stop, but as you are quite inconvenienced with a gag, I shall have to be the judge. Such an insolent and feisty little miss, aren't you? But then I wouldn't be enjoying myself so much if you were a tame one.'

Each crack of the crop made her wince: not the sting, the sting was exquisite. She had never felt pain before during sex, had always been dominant and controlled it all, and until this night, the thought of sex came second to most other things. She searched for the voice for a few seconds – wanting to tell it, to share the devilish torment she was enjoying so much.

'It will return just in time,' he answered her thought as he dropped the crop beside her on the bed. 'Now Miss, Daddy wants to slip inside that soft succulent mess he's made.' He grabbed both her arms pinning her harder on the bed and applying just enough pressure to keep them behind her back. He circled her opening with his hot cock, she tried pushing herself against it – wanting him in her, wanting him to cum in her and own her. He pushed her back, taking his time, rubbing her clit with his knob, then she felt the fully hard cock enter, his hard thighs against her ass – he began to move in her slowly, each grind harder and better than the last.

She was cumming so hard that she began to lose her breath, panic filled her, but not because she thought she would pass out, it was because she felt like she was dying, her whole-body orgasming to his touch. He fucked faster and pressed himself against her back, releasing her arms and sinking his teeth into her neck. She could feel his sweat on her body, it was sticky and hot, making them slip together more as he pumped harder and faster, his huge sack bouncing and slapping at her clit.

'Want Daddy's seed?' he growled in her ear as she felt his cock getting ready to burst. She nodded wildly, desperate for him to fill her.

He moaned loudly as his hot juice erupted, her back arching as she pressed herself hard against him. He forced her back down, gripping her buttocks, pulling them apart slightly so he could see her ass. At the same time, he penetrated it with his thumb, forcing himself deeper into her dark red cunt, his cum filling her and letting out a husky groan as he ejaculated. His grip was so intense on her hips that she sobbed; she had never felt so dominated.

He slipped out and pushed her away from him dismissively she reached for the gag and slid it down her neck.

'Get used to it there,' he said, toying with the silk material, and he got up and walked to the bar. 'A little nightcap?'

He didn't wait for an answer, fixing them both whiskey on the rocks and putting it beside her on the bed. 'I don't usually share my bed with anyone, for sleep that is, you follow? Now I could be a thorough cad and ask you to either leave or sleep on the more than adequate couch. Still, I shan't.' He tapped her nose again, which she girlishly enjoyed, and which also irritated her.

'I'm going to contract you for a full 48 hours if you agree you will be at my beck and call and every whim. Obviously, after 48 hours, I can't think of many that will have any use for you.' He laughed as he studied her face for reactions.

'At least not here, excuse me – I said that as if you would be maimed or worse. I own a fair portion of this city, and most would be reticent to solicit one of my conquests.'

He was stroking her hair, and her eyes began to drop. 'I think this one is ready for bed,' he said and slipped her legs beneath the sheets. 'Nighty night then, and no cussing me in your dreams – I think you have figured enough out to know that nothing gets passed me, and nothing is beyond me.'

She felt him get up off the bed, and buried her head in the plush pillows, drifting off into the deepest sleep. All she felt was the slow thump of her heartbeat, so slow it felt like it would stop making her sleep almost coma-like, and if that panicked her, she was too intoxicated to care.

The sweetest softest slumber fell upon her, a gentle hand stroked her face and temples. 'Crystal, Crystal, can I speak to Tuppence?'

Her body became warm, and her heartbeat steadied as a euphoria oozed around her pulses and erogenous zones, tickling her soul with black thoughts. She relaxed beneath the very sophisticated touch.

Little girl, such a tough little girl but treated right, so tender… I delight in the raw meats.

Your blood is so full of fire, I want, I need to taste it, savour it beneath my tongue. Swim in your beautiful state of tragedy. Let your tragedy out, girl, let me drink from you. You, not Crystal.

Crystal is a fake who hurts you always because she cannot

abide by the beauty of you. I would cherish you, Tuppence, I want you.

I want to own you, show you what you should be, let Daddy in, baby girl.

She groaned softly as the touch penetrated her lips, then traced a line back up the curves of her body until he let her taste herself.

See how sweet you are? Feel how much I desire you?

Her aching flower bloomed so thoroughly that her legs slipped open wider, and her body arched up. 'Ugh yes, I want it. Tuppence wants it.'

A dark shadow entered her sleep state, its voice hoarse and husky as she felt its hairs prickle her skin, bringing her nipples to arousal as its hard-hot body wrangled with hers. Its eyes like a beast.

It was muscular and dominant, she begged for it to enter her by rubbing her wet pussy against its massive hot member. She knew it was so wrong to enjoy it, but 'Fuck God!' she yelled, she was so turned on by the fear, by its claws and wet dripping fangs.

The hair over its body disgusted her, but that made her perversely even hornier. Its massive erect cock thick and long and hard. She could never take that, but oh god, she wanted it.

'Fuck, I'm so fucking wet for it. 'She felt herself pulling down the panties wanting the beast just to fuck her hard and right now, wanting it to hurt her, but why?

She reached for it grabbing it and feeling how hard and hot it was. So scared but beyond fear she'd ever known, this was primeval, so wrong and exquisite and made the aching so bad, needing to know what was beyond. She felt it claws hook her panties, already partly shredded and sliced them off. Her thighs were wet where it had been drooling. She was cumming so hard it felt like she would pass out with the anticipation of what was to come, her breath laboured, her heart pounding, feeling the rough tongue on her breasts.

It growled out loud, gripping her hips and moving its back legs in position to force its massive member inside her, grunting as it fucked her harder and harder, eating her mouth as she cried in orgasm. Her soft, supple thighs wrapped about its body, almost cosseting the beast to her.

It arched back baring its teeth, every muscle and vein in its body protruding as it began to cum inside her. It fucked her harder, lifting her off the bed, pounding and rocking into her, filling her tight muscles with hot cum. Its grip dug in so deep that she cried in a sweet agony and held on tighter with her thighs as its claw-like hands slid to the top of her arms to pin her.

It stroked longer and deeper in her then wildly, with an animal growl, turned her over, grabbing her soft ass and rubbing its firm cock against it.

It pushed her face down and made her ass come up high while its rough tongue took its pleasure, licking her tight muscle pushing inside it and lapping up the slit of the creamy cunt. Then almost without warning forced its rock-hard shaft in, her buttocks spreading and filling with its hard cock, roaring it fucked her like a beast, her body and soul were on fire, she wanted more pain, more beasting.

Tenderly she licked its claws on her arm and

tongued them as it began to climax in her, she wanted it to see how much she wanted it too. It bent low to breathe in her ear then sunk its shark teeth into her neck as its beautiful juice spilt out of her, pounding her ass feverishly. She was sweaty and sticky and more aroused and orgasmic than she'd ever felt, she screamed as the last of its cum filled her, and it howled wildly shuddering inside her.

Its grip left her, and she turned to take in its magnificence again, but it was gone, she tried to wake herself, but a deep enveloping spell fell upon her again.

Such a sweet and good girl, she heard as sleep took her, and the night came to own her. She rubbed her thighs together, still orgasming. Never once did she think it was wrong, never once did she look for forgiveness.

How could something so pleasurable be wrong?

CHAPTER 7

All she could make out was some shafts of light, through a black gauze. She went to move to remove it, but her body was asleep. Or was it?

She cried out as she yanked her arm, feeling something soft hold her back but restrictive. Her legs were held tight and sore, her neck bound so as if she moved too much, her breath stopped. She murmured through a soft gag, panic rising, tears blurring her sight, stinging her eyes.

The velvet voice of Robert Alexander whispered, 'Hush now, Baby girl, don't try to move, it wasn't my plan to hurt you, but if you keep struggling, soft will become harsh, and you so suit soft ties. Like a pretty little puppet doll.'

His finger traced a line down her face and skimmed over her proud breasts and thighs as she arched up to hear – to find some reason or more words from him to explain.

'Do you smell the coffee and croissants?' he softly said.

She flinched as the heat from the drink warmed her face, and the smell of the croissants made her feel sick, the fear taking away any pleasure from either.

'Silly me, there I was waiting for a response, and here I have you all tied up with no way of communicating apart from certain areas of your body.' His fingers stroked her nipple, circling it softy before skimming her slim waist, dipping between her splayed legs and caressing her clitoris. Her oozing juices betrayed what she thought and felt.

It's just panic, you vain cunt, she thought bitterly then stopped, knowing he could read her like a master.

'No, that's not panic, little one, that's fear and excitement – fear being a much under-rated sexual stimulant.'

She arched her body up to meet his touch again, the orgasms making her wildly crave his touch.

'Tut tut, you wanton hussy, Daddy's not quite ready for you yet.'

She felt his weight lift off the bed as his touch stopped, her hearing was so heightened that she heard every footstep of him walking away, she shivered, it was that sick adrenaline again.

She jerked as she heard a switch followed by music. It was choral but demonic – her breathing laboured again as he said, 'Mozart's Requiem, quite an evocative and powerful creation – as are you, you silly little thing. You see you think very little of yourself, that once your virginity was lost – I'm guessing around age eleven, that all your magic was gone. The only path for Tuppence oh I must apologise as I've used your given name instead of that silly tag, Crystal. Anyway, I digress, you see the very fact that you believe you have no magic is rather enticing to me. There is much treasure to be had from someone who's actual attractiveness is hidden beyond the surface. Though you're pretty! Goodness me, I almost forgot to tell you that, but it's not why I have brought you here.'

She felt him sit down on the bed again, his hand fished behind her head and released the gag around her mouth. She gasped for air; her mouth so dry she couldn't voice any words. 'Sip?' he said, holding the warm coffee by her mouth, 'Sip, or you'll choke, your mouth and throat are parched.'

She licked the rim of the cup and took a small mouthful as he tipped it gently — her lips were trembling as some of it slipped out of the sides.

'Oh dear, you've made a mess, let me fix that.'

She heard him put the coffee down and fish in his pocket, then he dabbed her mouth with a soft silky handkerchief. He was so terrifying but also tender, her heart was thumping wildly as he bent forward again. 'You've been such a good girl, do you mind me calling you Princess? I got the impression it had some significance, but of course, I may be over-attentive and reading too much in?'

She gasped and sobbed and felt disgusted. 'It's just my, no, it's fine, I just, I find it childish.' She was desperate to remove her father's image from her mind as his fingers stroked while she sputtered out the words.

She was disgusted by it and brutally blanked thoughts of her father, laughing bitterly.

'Cunt.'

'Who me? Oh dear, best we keep it as me, though I'm not fond of the name, we don't want any more incestuous thoughts ruining our little party.'

His words were like black magic. She wondered at how grown up she felt within seconds of him delivering them. She knew she needed, wanted to break away from the childish girl who always got hurt.

'Daddy,' she said breathily. 'You're my only Daddy.'

His hand massaged her wet cunt, making her ready to cum again. 'Such a receptive little thing and so reactive, it's intensely erotic and more virginal than any young thing thinking she's special.'

She felt his tongue on her hot clit for seconds, which made her want more.

'Patience, Daddy has such plans for you. You see, I want you to cum over the thought of me destroying you.' The words were spoken harshly but tickled her ears, his tongue flicking in and out of them, the feeling feathering down her throat and making her mouth water.

'Now then, I think a visit to the powder room is needed – let me assist.'

She went to speak, but her tongue and mouth were acting like they didn't belong to her, she managed a sob as he untied her hands and feet but left her neck,

'Are you going to fight me, miss? You feel this tiny little insignificant necktie I have on you? It's all I need to completely deactivate you.' He tugged it until she gasped for breath. 'Although I do enjoy a struggle – let's see, shall we? I do so savour the human spirit.' He untied it, and she immediately shot forward, jumping off the bed. Still, her legs were weak and gave beneath her, and as she stumbled to the floor, he laughed. 'Like releasing a springbok from a trap!'

She was trembling and dragged her legs up so as she was on all fours. 'Who the hell do you think... 'She stopped.

She knew she had enjoyed it, enjoyed the fear more than she'd ever want to say. She was still cumming - a soft, slow orgasm that kept tickling different parts of her body.

'Uh uh,' he said, grabbing her hands as they went to remove the blindfold. 'That's for Daddy to enjoy a bit later. First, we have to see to your toilette madam.'

He pulled her to her feet, his hard body pressed against hers. She was still weak though wickedly wanted more but knew if he knew he would stop. I know that much about you, Mister, she thought, always searching for the voice in her head.

'Ugh, tedious, obvious, I think you'll find that's bravado, I do wish you would stop the tiring and very annoying thoughts.' He moved her forward until her feet touched an icy cold floor which she recognised as the bathroom. 'Just a few steps more,' he said, then sat her down on the toilet. 'Go on then, I can shower and bathe you after, as for makeup we won't bother with that until I've finished my little game. Then you can see to yourself as I plan to take you out tonight, such a fortunate girl, don't you think?'

She heard him walk a few steps and stop,

'You must need to pee urgently; your belly is protruding ever so slightly. Why are you keeping me waiting? Do you think it is alluring?'

She knew his eyes were on her and felt so cheap and couldn't hold on much longer.

You bastard, she thought but decided to just release her bladder even with him watching.

'Good girl,' he said as a stream of piss leaked from her body. She felt herself blush, which made her angry.

Damn, she really did not want him to notice.

'Ah, Daddy's little girl is feeling embarrassed? It's ok, we all need to pee.'

She finished, anger and frustration welling up inside her at the humiliation. Still, she was also strangely getting off on it. She heard him walking towards her, he handed her tissues and didn't move until she had finished wiping herself. His hand softly took hers, leading her to the sink to wash her hands, then from the bathroom, he gently pushed her onto the edge of the bed and made her lay back. She reached for the blindfold immediately hearing a whoosh sound before the shocking pain.

'Don't you dare,' he hissed in her ear as her hands instinctively moved to protect her under the breast which he had just savagely caught with the crop or whip, something vicious. She froze, his voice chilling her blood.

'I will throw you out on the street as you stand if you disobey me again so as everyone can see the whore that you are. No, hands above your head.'

'Arrogant cunt,' she mouthed silently, her mind spinning with rage excitement and pleasure, but something inside was screaming for her to leave, to get out.

Was it the voice?

'Going to fuck you so hard, Baby girl. Make you scream like you've never screamed before or will ever experience again. You're mine to do with as I wish! Do you understand the rules?'

'Yes … I think.'

A sharp pain shot through her nerves as he expertly and harshly pinched the soft, delicate, and painful fleshy skin under her arm. Calmly and softly, he whispered in her ear, 'I am offering to train, spend my time and take you places no one else will ever be able to retake you, so listen carefully young lady and think about your reply. I ask you once more, and once more only, Crystal, do you understand the rules?'

Her mind racing, part of it telling her to run while she still felt she had the luxury of choice but another part thinking,

God yes, I want this. I want some luxury for a while, and all I must do is let him fuck me and do some kinky shit. Come on then you filthy rich bastard, show me your worst.

She felt him stand. 'No answer, huh? I will call the limo for you, and you can go, actually a taxi as you've done nothing yet to warrant a ride.'

Crystal dropped forward off the bed on to her knees, not wanting to lose out now after all he had put her through. 'Yes Daddy, I understand, you can do anything with me, Daddy. Yes, Daddy, I agree, please train me, don't throw me out I beg you.'

He was silent and still.

Christ, what do I do?

The usual tricks she used on men would never work here, not with this giant of a man. She avoided grabbing his cock to pleasure him, though that was her instinct.

Why can't he be like all the other fuckers and just need their cock played with and sucked, then I'd be winning again.

She was on all fours, reaching for his shoes and humiliating herself, but strangely didn't find it so difficult. Had his treatment of her raised her threshold nshe wondered, as her hands touched them? She would have to beg and had never done that before, except in play.

Why the fuck am I doing this?

Her thoughts screamed. *Bastard, you cunt! You know I need this.*

She felt herself blush instinctively knowing he could read her, but then she smiled, thinking she did it all the time.

'You just give 'em the options to what you already have all the answers to,' she accidentally let slip. 'I'm sorry, Daddy, please forgive me. I was thinking about I... again. I am not worthy of your training, please do with me whatever you want. I.... I mean whatever you feel I need or deserve.'

She could not believe how hot it made her feel, she could only imagine it was that she wasn't in control.

I'm not fucking subbing myself, mind. Fuck no, this is special, not just some cheap kink.

It made her wet, giving herself away to a stranger and becoming a slave to whatever he wanted.

Oh God, she thought. *This is so fierce.*

She felt his hand on her head, stroking her hair. He bent down and pulled her up, spinning her around, her hands grabbed for him to steady herself. Still, he slapped them away and pushed her back down. 'Just admiring my acquisition from every possible angle.'

He leaned forward, his breath on her ear so calm and controlled. Moments passed.

Fuck, have I missed what he said to me? Her mind panicked, and she felt her lips quiver, then he spoke, words spoken slowly and for her to clearly understand.

'Crystal, never forget your words or your respect again! Because if you do, there will be no second chance with me. I do not play those games and WILL NOT ever accept it from you or any other female who wants to learn from me. Indeed, she must offer me her body and soul and mind, the whole package is what makes Daddy smile, sweetheart. I will treat you well while you are with me, you will want for nothing,' he grabbed a handful of her hair and pulled her head back, 'except sometimes maybe my mercy.'

He sat her down, and she felt his weight next to her, gently he lifted the coffee back to her lips, saying, 'Sip this, remember it is still hot.'

As he fed her, his gentleness and concern were overwhelming. Crystal found herself close to tears as he stroked her back through the luxurious cotton dressing gown. She felt her eyes fill with tears and hated herself for it, showing her weakness for him was the last thing she wanted to do. It was the last thing she gave up, he had her. She swallowed hard as he softly wiped away the tears from her cheeks, tender hands, pulling her to her feet again. 'I think you need some relief,' he said cryptically, removing her tiny robe.

'No, no, I am fine, Daddy, surely this breakfast and gentle treatment is enough?'

He caressed her fingertips with the crop, 'Is that defiance? Baby girl, I thought we had this covered, either back down or is this your way of telling me that you want more? Hmm?' I think I prefer the latter scenario.'

He pressed her against the wall. 'Hush now, not a word.'

She heard the crop fly through the air as he whipped her ass, the pain making her cry out, but then the feathery strokes began to make her wet and throb with the burn, the humiliation. The second stinging strike from his crop took her unawares after the soft touches that had followed the first. She let out a cry of pain and pleasure, immediately his hand was on the back of her neck, pulling her hair.

'Not a word, remember? Or do you want more? And you needn't worry about being marked for tonight's excursion, Daddy knows how to administer punishment without leaving a trace to spoil your look.'

He gently guided the crop over her buttocks. She knew there was more to come and was, again, annoyed at herself for finding this treatment such a turn on.

The crop struck hard, and Crystal buttocks felt as though a flame had been drawn across them. She heard her master's voice again in her ear. 'Crystal, you will count each stroke until ten, that was one, let me hear you and remember your respect to Daddy.'

'One, thank you, Daddy,' she announced with a mixture of sexual lust and fear.

'Good girl,' was all Daddy said to her before the next strike lit up her buttocks.

'Two, thank you, Daddy.' She carried on counting, but as number five struck her, she began to cry, biting hard on her lip so as not to show it.

'Five Daddy, thank you, but please show me mercy?'

With a firm grip on her hair again, Robert Alexander leaned in. 'You dare ask me for mercy? That has just added two more for you to keep count of. Shall we say this is a training guide, a sanction to prevent you from slipping again.'

He tightened his grip on her hair as the crop flew through the air again. Crystal bit on her arm, her body tensed and ready to receive his strokes. Her buttocks screamed to be moved out of the way. The crack made her scream to herself, but where was the pain? Hate seethed in her as she realised he had played her. She began to turn, but his grip on her hair stopped any movement.

Before she reached out to scratch his hand holding her, she felt number six harsher across her ass and realised he had played her again. He had caught her off guard, she knew she had no choice now, her relaxed buttocks brought her butt into a subversive role with the pain that shot through her body.

Her mind raced, but the pain and complete domination were exquisite. She cried through her tears. 'Six Daddy, thank you,' hating herself for reacting so primitively and biting back.

You fucking bastard, I'd fucking kill anyone who hit me before you came along! Don't fuck my mind up, you total cunt. Hate you!

Robert Alexander dealt another four painful cracks across her buttocks, making her wait with torturing anticipation for each one.

She pushed back from the wall but was firmly put back against it by him. His grip on her hair had not lessened.

'You've fucking hit me ten times, that's its Mister …. Daddy.'

'Oh, but Crystal, have you forgotten your punishment for not following the rules? Hmm?'

Robert Alexander looked directly into Crystal's tearful red eyes; she had so hoped that those two spanks would be forgotten but should have known better. Reluctantly she assumed her position against the wall, pushing her buttocks out slightly.

'Crystal these last four are going to hurt, they are a punishment. Do you understand? It hurts Daddy more than it does you.'

'Yes, Daddy, I understand, but … but Daddy, wasn't it just two?'

'Indeed. Indeed, it was. Good girl for listening. Two it is then.'

Crystal's body quivered uncontrollably; the anticipation was unbearable.

When? She thought, which was answered with the crop across her rear, which made her eyes roll back and she thought she would pass out. The pain was awful, and still, another to come. The pleasure side of this experience had vanished for Crystal, overtaken with a desire to serve or please her master, her Daddy. She knew this last one was going to be the worst and tried to ready herself by telling herself to relax.

Her voice began taunting her.

This is what you want, huh? You stupid bitch. You fucked up big time with this one, he is gonna beat you, use you and then throw you out onto the streets like the tramp you are. You need to stick him you fucking waste of egg and spunk before he dumps your fucked-up body, stick him, and grab what you can.

NO! I will earn out of this. Just FUCK OFF and leave me alone, you cunt! I hate the way...

Crystal couldn't finish the answer haunting her mind before the final harsh full-powered strike hit her, causing her to burst into tears and begin sliding down the wall. She tried so hard to stand, but her body had had enough, and her legs buckled. All she could do was call out, 'Daddy. Daddy'

She had no other words. She was scared to speak in case she got it wrong and was given more guidance from him. He grabbed her, scooping her legs and upper back and lifted her into his arms. She instinctively hugged him for comfort but was terrified he'd push her away. He allowed it as he carried her to the bathroom, sat her gently on a seat, and began to run it.

The steam-filled her senses and aroused parts of her she didn't know existed, it was deliciously perfumed with spices and heady scents. With no effort at all, he picked her up. He slipped her into the luxurious bath, initially stinging her buttocks but slowly soothing the pain. His fingers stroked her shoulders and massaged them lightly as he began to soap her.

His breathing was passionate and made her feel hotter, wanting him to lose it and just fuck her wildly. He spent time working her shoulders and upper back, and she accepted his softness eagerly, hoping it would not be spoilt by any harshness.

He whispered into her ear, 'I want you to relax and enjoy this, put yourself in my hands and let me pleasure your body which has worked so hard.'

The massage relaxed her, she felt the tension lift from her body and lost time, it just felt so good. Robert Alexander moved from her back and began massaging the nape of her neck and head, it was sheer bliss to her, total heaven as he gave her the full works.

Cradling her head above the water, he soaked her hair. He began washing it, his stiff fingers sensuously rubbing her scalp. His fingers moved down to her breasts, rubbing erotically without touching her begging nipples. She gasped as she arched up, trying to force him to touch them, and his response was to push her further down. He submerged his hands in the bath, stroking her abdomen and skimming her pussy.

'Please Daddy, Just dip in. Ugh, I need you to stop the ache.'

He pulled her thighs apart softly and let one finger slip in between her lips, she raised her hips to capture the delicious feeling of the finger in her deeply.

'No baby girl, I need you to anticipate not predict or guide.'

He went to the foot of the bath and lifted her foot to his mouth gently tonguing her toes and massaging her calves firmly, his thumb went to her arch and pressed deeply sending relaxing pleasure up her leg relaxing and soothing her,

'Dancers have such sensitive feet,' he said as he rubbed each part of her foot with his beautifully manicured hands then continued pampering her desperate body. He asked for her hand and helped her stand, watching the water runoff her body before him. He studied her for a few seconds that felt like an eternity before he reached for a large fluffy towel and wrapped her in it as he helped her out of the bath.

Sitting her back on the seat, she winced a little, reminded immediately of the thrashing she had received earlier. It was so sore she had to sit more on her thighs than her buttocks, even putting her hands underneath her for some respite. He reached for another towel with which he dried her hair, then discarding this over the bath he led her to the bedroom.

She heard him removing his clothes, her heart was racing – she'd never wanted to be fucked so hard in all her life. He took her hand and stroked it against his cock, 'I expected this game to last far longer, you know,' he said flippantly.

It was exactly what she needed, he'd been so harsh, and she needed to hear softness.

Sliding behind her, he ripped her blindfold off and pushed her forward aggressively face down on the bed.

'Oh god, just fuck me, please – I need you in me so bad, Daddy, 'she screamed. His full weight went behind her, and his hard cock entered her roughly. He said nothing but she loved it – she wanted more of it, wanted more danger. His teeth bit down hard on her shoulder, and he began to fuck harder and faster, his body pressed against hers, his hot cock slipping in and out of her wet cunt.

Every thrust hurt her buttocks, but she found the pain such a turn on.

He grabbed her hair until she screamed as he filled her with his cum, yanking her to the side with one leg over his shoulder, his face wild with arousal, and his eyes jet black with passion. He fucked her cum-filled pussy until he let out a deep groan, his grip digging into her hip as he released from his tightened sac again.

'Ugh, Daddy, ugh god yeah, I love you fucking me, you cunt,' she cried, cumming over every inch of him.

He pushed her forward off him. 'Naughty girls get the gag again if they return to the vernacular in Daddy's presence.'

He spanked her hard and got off the bed, watching his magnificent form as he grabbed a towel and wrapped himself in it. She eyed him lustfully, wanting to feel more fear, wanting him to take the places that terrified her.

'Now you can see to yourself, I'm off out for the day but will return around seven, be ready – I've set some things out for you.'

'Huh?' she said and told herself off for sounding so stupid.

'Yes, you do sound rather stupid, miss. The instructions are plain, surely?'

She sat back down on the bed, embarrassed to move, for him to watch her – she would wait until he left, she thought, she wanted to see what he had bought her but not to sound like an idiot by gushing.

She was now so unsure how to act again when only five minutes back, it had been primate and instinctive.

It was too confusing for her and so languished on the bed until she heard the lift ping and Robert Alexander leave.

CHAPTER 8

SHE TOWELLED HER HAIR AGAIN AND DECIDED TO WRAP the one he had used around her. She could smell him on it - his cologne, his musk.

'*Idiot,*' the voice whispered spitefully. '*What do you think this is a romantic comedy? You the quirky schizophrenic nutcase that wins over the property mogul? If that's what he is, you obsessive little cunt.*'

She cringed at its words. The voice was pure evil at times, not always, but that was generally for the setup and ensuing poison. She hummed to herself tenderly, trying to ignore it, but she knew it still hung around and would until she responded.

'*Why don't you fuck off, you're just jealous. After all, you only live because I do, and if you ever place me in real danger, then you're just as screwed, hmm? Now get fucked your pathetic freak.*'

She was pleased with that put down and true to form she silenced the inner voice but not before letting her know that she didn't control it. As much as she hated it, she also depended on it.

'You're a sad and lonely fucked up little girl.'

Skipping to the bed, she eyed the clothes he had set out. Daddy had set out a tiny Levi tee and jeans, converse pumps, but no lingerie. She quickly checked about for her clothes but couldn't see them anywhere.

'How the fuck do I wear that tee with no bra? Typical male!'

She dried herself off and slipped into what he had bought her, the tee was a little snug, but it fitted well – maybe too well, she thought as her breasts were showcased just like a hooker would wear it.

'Also, Mister, it's the freakin' winter! I'm going to freeze my tits off, and the tee will kinda make that apparent. Jeez, I guess I'm staying in then.'

She stopped as she caught sight of the couch, a black leather biker style jacket draped across the back and a merino scarf that she ran to and snuggled to her face. G

rabbing the coat and smelling the new leather, she caressed it, saying, 'Well alright then. I guess you did think after all.'

She grabbed her bag, which thankfully he hadn't disposed of, and removed a spare mascara, lippy and a little bronzer, applying it quickly before heading for the lift. She took a glance at the full-length mirrors in the lift and smiled to herself as the leather jacket accentuated her breast through the white cotton tee.

As the doors opened, she gazed furtively at the receptionist.

'Good morning miss – I trust you slept?' he finished with a laugh, but she flicked her hair and flipped him the finger, skipping down the steps to find the limo was waiting for her.

The driver was standing by the passenger door, and as she got closer, he opened it for her.

'It's ok, I'll walk, it's such a lovely day. Just give me the address.' Crystal said to the driver.

'No Miss, you are to get in the limo, and I am to ensure I get you there in time,' he replied, looking at Crystal with a little concern.

Crystal knew the driver was not going to share where she was meeting Robert Alexander, so reluctantly climbed into the limo.

'Thank you, Miss,' said the driver as he closed the door.

THE RIDE WAS ABOUT FIFTEEN MINUTES, ENDING ON A café lined street.

The door opened, and the driver offered his hand to help her exit the vehicle. The hum hit her, of ladies who brunched squawking with their high-pitched laughter and waiters pandering to their vanities.

'Miss, you need to arrive at L'Agneau d'Or within the next ten minutes, just a little further along the street,' he said. 'Don't be late, Miss.'

Crystal thanked the driver as he walked off, closing the door and driving off.

'Voulez Vous. I like the look,' she whispered to herself as she took in the bistro chairs and tables outside and the smell of the French coffee. 'Maybe I'll keep you waiting, Mr, just a little diversion.'

She giggled to herself, not thinking and was caught up in the luxurious time she was spending.

Most tables were taken; in fact, it was heaving as she tried to make her way through without hitting someone. She had always been a clumsy girl and had failed driving tests five times, with the instructor saying she had the worst hand-eye coordination he had ever seen,

Though he didn't complain, she smiled to herself, when she wanked him off and gave him a blowjob for those free lessons.

She shook the thought out of her mind as she remembered the sweaty, pissy smell and taste of his tiny cock. Strangely she could dance, at least she could move, but only to music. She had always loved music - any beat or sound would bring out the Diva in her.

Several guys noticed her boobs and hard nipples in the tight tee as the wind blew her biker jacket open. She kinda liked it, and it showed. One asked her to sit with them, but she replied, 'No thanks, Sunday mornings are just for me.' She enjoyed the putdown. 'Cunt.' she said as she passed him. 'I hooked me a begun'!'

'You're sure? Hooked?' she thought she heard but carried on annoying people who were enjoying their coffee, by elbowing and apologising.

'Madam.' The dark oily waiter accosted her. 'A table?'

She scanned about her. 'Oh, my fucking goodness, he's here!' And there he was, sat abreast one of the most stunning blondes she had ever seen.

He sipped an espresso while this gorgeous animal fell all over him, lean, lithe limbs and a full E Cup stretched out across him, fondling and kissing him. He dismissed it, though, smiled and pulled her beautiful flaxen hair from her neck, planting a soft kiss and pinching her nose.

'That's me, for fuck's sake!' she barked, as the waiter ushered her to a table next to them. 'Thanks, just coffee and a croissant if that's ok?'

She dismissed him, unable to take her eyes from Robert Alexander.

You fucking dick, fuck you! She thought as she sat down, trying to avert her ardent gaze.

'*You sad fucking bitch!*' the voice viciously sniped back. '*You can't compete. You're pretty yeah, but she's all the fucking stars, fuck off back to the gutter or do something so wild that none of them can match!*'

She shuddered at its viciousness, but that was always the way, and she knew it produced results, nobody knew her as it did. She had run from a section because of this strange and dark voice.

A friend had sent her an email while on section 3 for outrageous and wild behaviour. Her family had had enough of her rolling in after weekends away drinking and sleeping around.

The email had attached an ad placed in The London Herald.

'Little Bird of Paradise Wanted for The Cage, our kittens need new meat.'

There was a PO Box and a photo requirement

though it said just to turn up and impress and not to expect a response.

The Collared Kitten was given as the address, nothing more, so she had figured although it was probably a secret club, word on the street would take her there.

It made her blood throb around her body in a heady heat. It had to be dancing, and although she had the worst coordination for most things, she could always move. Her parents had enrolled her in ballet, tap, and gymnastics at an early age to try to rectify her wayward and accident-prone manner. At least on the dance floor, she was accomplished and followed instruction. However, a little improvisation always delighted those who taught her.

This fuelled her already heightened adrenaline, and that day, while day release patients were walking out, she escaped and joined a party of visitors as they talked about their relatives and how well they seemed to be doing. She smiled sweetly pretending to be a nurse, even asking for a light and stopping at the gates, she knew she had to look confident though her heart raced out of her chest.

She made it and left Salisbury on the first train knowing not much fuss would be made as there were always escapees.

Every attempt to talk to her that day, as she journeyed to London, fuelled paranoia. At one point, she became so stressed that she left the train to catch another just to be rid of the attention from a group of lads asking for her number.

Her mind flicked back to where she was, her eyes though glazed over, had not left the table where he sat with the Fucking Skanky Witch that had his attention.

You sick cunt, like he wanted you for anything more than a quick fuck,' the voice laughed wickedly in her ear, and a sob caught in her throat as she gazed at the feline creature about him.

She was everything Crystal wasn't. She was pure confidence, not adrenaline and class, speaking and giggling like the sound of bees on a warm summer's day.

She made up her mind to leave just as the waiter brought her order. 'No thanks, I'm going. What?' she sharply snapped at him, 'I haven't eaten or drank, so I'm sure as fuck not paying!'

She felt humiliated, and something in her always wanted to increase that state when it happened, as if being the worst in a crowd somehow took away the sting. She wanted to disgust everyone around her and eyed many as they began to laugh. At that moment, the group of men walked in.

'Here!' one shouted. 'Hey there, I'll fetch her bill, what an absolute refreshing delight!' He was handsome, but nobody took her attention from Robert. The latter ran his fingers through his hair and leaned back in his chair, 'Patience baby girl,' he pointedly said to her.

'Here!' he tapped the chair opposite him and whispered to the blonde who was trying to mask her snobby laugh at Crystal with fake admiration as she watched his reaction.

Her deep blue eyes lowered, and she shrugged her

shoulders while elegantly raising herself from the table. 'Sweetheart, I have everything I could want in life and have tried most things but excuse me if I skip your humiliation. Enjoy,' she bitterly added and left as Robert Alexander tapped her on the ass.

Crystal sniggered as she fumbled and sat down opposite him ungainly, blushing and choking on her laugh.

'I find sniggering incredibly unattractive,' he flatly said, which made her even more nervous. 'Unless of course it's followed by even more, then I can't help but wonder what it is that is so funny? And if the subject of the humour is said sniggering person, then I always say that humiliation on another can be quite amusing, even sexually arousing?'

'I'm quite sure I dunno what you are on about, Mr.'

'Daddy, please,' he stroked her trembling hand with his finger but wasn't affection. It was a warning.

'What the fuck, even in public?' she choked out.

'In any other situation, and with anyone inferior to yours truly, that faux pas would be a tad embarrassing. But as you see, nobody here is interested in your dramatics you disappear to all except me.'

He hailed the waiter. 'Get this little minx a nice fruity white not too dry as she's a little hoarse and we don't want any more choking, at least not in public.'

The waiter dipped a little and turned to go. 'One more thing, my little oily French friend, something to eat as she has a hard day ahead of her. What would you suggest?'

The waiter puffed out his chest, 'Monsieur Alexander, I am honoured that you seek my humble opinion.'

'Damn it, I'm not sure I want to know, seeing as you call it humble, just the wine and a menu then and no more grovelling you tiring little sycophant.'

He neither laughed at nor acknowledged the effect as the waiter stumbled his way through the crowd shouting at a waitress to bring a menu to them and blushing furiously.

Robert Alexander was still stroking her hand as she mulled over the last ten minutes. 'Mr err, Daddy, I wish you wouldn't touch me like that. See that's not right to show affection but mean something else.'

'And who says I mean anything other than affection? It's just my particular type of affection which up until now you seem to have been enjoying, hmm?'

He took his hand away and sat back in his chair eyeing her, she giggled,

'Preferable to the snigger,' he remarked, which she lapped up still hungry for his emotional assault.

She knew she was addicted and knew that sick n sweet tenderness always followed a gut-wrenching attack.

The wine came with the waitress, Crystal gulped it down. 'Another? Or would you rather we took this somewhere else? More private, where Daddy can lick your wounds and make his little girl smile again, hmm? Such a sad little face you are wearing and, no scratch that, I'm not interested in your smile, I like this.'

His hand slid beneath the table and travelled up her

thighs, unzipping her jeans. She opened them as his finger delved into her jeans and wet knickers.

'Normally, I enjoy quashing rebellion, but I have to say your resistance is hugely attractive to me. And before you go to explain your presence here as opposed to where instructed, I guessed and am delighted with myself that I knew you would be here.'

'Ugh, Daddy,' she groaned softly as he toyed with her voluptuous clit. He slid his hand out again and closed her legs.

'Perfect little whore,' he whispered and got up, taking her arm in a gentlemanly fashion and pulling her beside him.

Nobody looked or noticed them leave, not because he wasn't magnificent. Still, she knew even then that it was because he owned them, if not through finance, through his presence and power.

The short walk back to the apartment was unnervingly quiet. H

er breaths were short and panicky, anticipating his dominant sex and unsure where it would or how it would end, but she couldn't run. She felt tethered, and every time she felt him jerk it, she came, came so hard it scared her. He stroked the back of her neck as the lift was called, gently moving her inside. His touch was so soft but entirely controlling as it ventured down her spine, dipping in her knickers and stroking the curve of her ass. A s the doors opened, he pushed her in aggressively onto the couch. She stayed face down, sobbing a little, as she heard him remove his belt.

He pulled her jeans and panties off roughly. 'I want the tee left on,' he said as he yanked her towards his hard thighs and cock. 'You think you're not a sweet girl, but Daddy knows different. Daddy wants to fuck your innocence.'

He grabbed her hair and yanked her head back, her body arching and trying to steady herself. Still, he wanted to fuck her uncontrollably and wanted her to lose balance, be unnerved. He held her only by her hair as his hard cock entered her wet cunt, she screamed as it hurt a bit, but his hand sought her mouth, and his thumb found its way in, 'Suck it, tongue it, you fucking slut.' Her tongue wildly circled and sucked it as he aggressively moved in her, humping her with every cry.

He pulled her to him, and his other hand went around her throat, his teeth sinking into the top of her bum cheeks.

'Ugh yeah, no I can't cum like this!' she cried, his grip tighter as she began to struggle to breathe. 'You will cum for me however I fucking want,' he said as his teeth bit down hard, drawing blood which he sucked up and savoured, saying she tasted sweet. That little moment of release from him made her so soft inside. Still, she knew that that was what he wanted as his cock jerked inside her, devouring her vulnerability.

'Daddy is so pleased with you.' He sounded strained as he began to fill her with his hot cum. 'So very pleased.'

It was a short hot and hard fuck, and she came so much she lost all sense of self as his juice leaked from her swollen wet pussy. She felt him arch up again, and a feeling of aggressive dominance entered her.

I got you now, Mr, she thought, which increased her pleasure until she forgot she wasn't breathing, his grip fierce on her throat.

Grabbing his hand and clawing at it to release her, she heard his deep laugh as his fingers loosened. He stroked where he had dug as he pushed her forward, releasing the last of his cum over her ass, pulling her cheeks apart to allow all of it to go everywhere. She knew he was watching as she turned to face him, she couldn't meet his eyes; they were too powerful, she felt them traverse her curves and whore like state. She wanted to speak but felt awkward.

He grabbed her up towards him rolling her hips against his. 'Get some rest,' he said, pushing her away.

She stumbled onto all fours and heard him laugh again. 'I'll just go to bed then, huh?' she scrambled to her feet loving every evil bit of it and felt him retake her hair and drag her to the bed.

'Dirty fucking little slut, that's just plain slutty,' he pushed her to the bed face down. 'Daddy so enjoyed your feeling of triumph, no point in a conquest if there's nothing to conquer, hmm?'

She flushed bright red and hid her face in the pillow. 'Wow I'm awful tired, you're right, I should sleep.'

He turned from her running his fingers through his hair and stroking his chest. 'Best get to it then. I have some work to do, and as enticing as you are, I'd rather wait to savour you.'

He was at the lift, she so wanted him to come back; she wanted to feel his softness, even if it meant another brutal attack. But that was it, and he left without saying anything. And, though she hated it, it's what she craved.

'Top session, you're all mine for the finishing, 'Daddy.' She laughed into the pillow and rolled around on the luxuriant bedding, 'Poor Daddy.'

She fell into a pleasant but dark deep sleep, satiated on her Daddy's sexing and orgasming softly, still feeling where he had been.

'You fucked up girl, you will always be my princess, but you have ruined your life, there is no coming back from this. Mum won't have you again, your brother and sisters won't visit you here and want nothing to do with you, they're disgusted and said they could never trust you around any of their kids. Still, I will protect you as best I can. I can't desert you as I feel partly responsible. I made you into a machine and now think you're the most unnatural thing I ever looked upon. One saving grace is that you have courage, maybe foolish, but it's there, and that will carry you through much in life, but that temper of yours has always been your problem, princess. I can't take responsibility for that, you were born screaming at the world, and that never stopped.

'That girl at school, she is scarred for life because of your temper, why the face Tuppence, why?'

The tears in her father's eyes always burnt her soul so deeply, and she could never forgive herself for the pain she caused him.

The girl at school had taken a picture of her father, torn from a family photograph, and threatened to flush it down the toilet. She had been bullying her for weeks and Tuppence, usually untouchable, had snapped. She couldn't remember what she had done to her as her mind had clouded over, but her face as the teachers, three of them, dragged her from her tormentor whose hair was still held tightly between her fingers. Blood over the bullies' face, in her hair and on the shard Tuppence had slashed her with. She was unable to remember how many times, just the screaming and other girls running from her.

The teachers struggled to control her and happily passed over control to the police on their arrival.

She was placed in juvenile detention until sixteen, and under the scrutiny of psychiatric professionals, was deemed a danger to society. Upon release, she was placed in the care of the community mental health team. She would be allowed to live a relatively healthy life but would never be rid of the pills or constant check-ups.

She soon got her hustler mind around the restrictions. She began her wild child life, drinking heavily and sleeping around until her father had had enough and asked for her to be sectioned.

She shuddered in her sleep as she remembered her last words to him. 'You sad old cunt, I'll be out before you know it and then I'll die Saracen you and the rest of them.'

Two days later, he was rushed to hospital with chest pains, her mother refused her admittance, and her father died of a heart attack before she got to say she was sorry.

Now 21, she hadn't seen or heard from any of them since, and she sobbed bitterly in her sleep, clutching her stomach, the tears soaking the pillows and her hair.

She felt an enveloping warmth as if arms around her and called out to her father, but it wasn't him. She knew it as she began to orgasm again and felt her legs gently pushed open.

'I'm your Daddy now, girl,' she heard in her sleep and felt her arms get pinned above her head. It was exactly what she needed, and she groaned as the dream took hold of her, her body and mind succumbing to every potent touch her twisted mind gifted her.

'You're my Daddy, Mr,' she cried as she came hard. 'Yeah, you're all I want.'

CHAPTER 9

'Ah, Daddy, that was such a sweet sleep,' she groaned as she awoke from her orgasmic slumber and reached over to touch him, but he wasn't there.

'Oh, huh! Silly me was just the bathrobe.'

Stupid cunt. Oh, Daddy this and Daddy that... you're just a shag, or whatever he chooses, the voice sniggered.

Oh, Daddy would just hate that you ugly prick. See, he's training me and hates sniggering, oh, and you know what? When I'm with him, I don't hear your voice or see your dark, decrepit shadow.

She smugly wrapped herself in his robe, delighted to have put the nasty little crippling voice down.

She stretched out her arms and felt a piece of paper. It was sealed in red wax and addressed to Tuppence. Before she could open it, she saw a beautiful dress and shoes laid out on the bed.

'Huh, no underwear again, Daddy? I'll have to be careful in that little number!' She squealed as she held the clothes to her and slipped on the shoes tearing open the note.

Tuppence, tonight is your night. See you at seven.

She held it to her nose, breathing deeply to try and take in his scent and leapt off the bed.

'*Hey, you! Yeah, you!*' she said as the dark wispy shadow of the voice appeared. '*I think he likes me!*'

'*Baby girl, he's hooked – while you slept, his fingers were all over your body, each curve measured with his incredibly experienced fingertips. He, he even licked, tasted, he couldn't get enough.*'

She held the dress in front of her, enjoying the capitulation of the voice. She knew this was always planned and always short-lived.

'I have to bath and eat, oh my, I'm so hungry, but oh, no, maybe not as it might anger Daddy? He said he's going to feed me tonight.

I'm so glad you conceded and delighted that you saw him do those things to me in my sleep, or else I would not have known, you disgusting little pervert. Know what else? I hear ya, and I'll tell ya that he is the one and that he feels the same way about me.

Ignoring the cynical, sinister laugh, it let out she skipped to the bathroom, grabbing her makeup, she stopped. 'No, he wouldn't, would he?' She ran back to the bed and grabbed up a silk purse, throwing its contents onto the bed.

'Oh, wow! Chanel makeup!' She ran to a box at the side of the bed, labelled, 'Wear me.'

'Chanel Mademoiselle, oh Daddy, you're the kindest. I wondered, I wondered at your harshness towards me but then thinks that's just us, that's our kink and you're right, I am enjoying it. I never felt so alive. Am I Alice to you? Ha, I say that because of the note 'Wear me?'

She rolled around on the bed for a few luxurious moments, cooing at her conquest.

'Nutcase, you fucking nutcase, you're scary. I like it.'

'Oh, shut up, you, see Daddy and I are all set up, and I'll never see or hear your wicked little jealous voice ever again.'

She stuck out her ass and tongue and ran to the bathroom. *'I have a whole two hours, I'm gonna make you so proud Daddy.'*

She stopped for a moment, sitting on the toilet pensively.

'Oh no, not that way. I'm not obsessed, I promise, and that's why you spank me, isn't it Daddy? Because before I've been too much and maybe, well, it sure doesn't matter now for you would never allow it.

Silly girl,' she whispered and hugged her waist as though in pain.

She stroked the marble bath as the hot scented bubbles began to fill her senses with a relaxing heady smell of the east. She slipped out of his bathrobe, reluctantly touching it one more time to her face, giggling as the hot water tickled her body, filling and lapped up around every curve.

She relaxed back and stroked her hair from her face. Her fingers strayed to her throat; she was cumming again as she'd never known, and she arched back moaning and tickling it further.

Her gentle fingers strayed to her rosebud nipples that were aroused. She circled them, enjoying the feeling of the velvet nobs, unlike her man who enjoyed hurting, biting, and pinching them till she squealed.

She cried out, raising her thighs and opening her legs at the thought of him. Still, her soft touch was strangely empty and irritated her a little, so she dug her nails in hard, her pale flesh rippling under her talons which made her yelp in pain.

'No! I'm not Daddy. He likes me soft and vulnerable.'

She shivered and went back to her soft way of stroking and raised her body as she began to cum, her fingers desperate to touch her clit.

Why should I wait? She thought. *I'm not Daddy, and this way, it keeps him unique. Fucks sake.*

She groaned despairingly. 'I just realised I'm doing that baby voice again, nope not going there this time. I'm Crystal and have no past.'

She slipped her hands between her legs and began to rub and finger her wet cunt, moaning, sniggering again, and chastising herself even though Daddy had told her off for that. She was a noisy girl and worried for a few seconds that the neighbours might hear but laughed because this was the penthouse, and Daddy didn't have any neighbours. Her wet pussy enveloped her thumb as her fingers wrapped the lower cheeks of her ass. She brought herself to orgasm again, and again, cheekily whispering, 'Don't worry, Daddy, it's nothing compared to you. I'm just so hot and horny and just want you here. I miss you, Daddy.' she sobbed and wiped her eyes with her wet fingers.

Cunt, you'll wish he wasn't pretty soon.

'Oh, fuck off you pervert,' she retaliated and grabbed a warm towel, standing shakily in the bath after climaxing so hard.

Her skin was soft and supple but made more so as Daddy had left some oils with a note saying, 'I WANT YOU TO SLIP INTO SOMETHING COMFORTABLE.'

She massaged herself sensuously, always feeling him, her flesh on fire, and her erogenous zones performing to her touch and thought. She walked to the dressing room mirror and splayed out the contents of the makeup bag.

Applied the tinted moisturiser and blush highlighted her cheekbones and brushed the dark, almost black eyeshadow across her orbital bones. Heavy black eyeliner and intense mascara finished the look with a sweep of dark rose heavily moisturised lipstick to her cupid's bow.

She kissed the mirror then scrawled on it, LOVE YOU, MY DADDY, singing to herself and grabbing up the delicious dress.

She slipped into its figure-hugging cling and stood admiring herself, the crest of her soft firm ass could be seen but not where Daddy had punished her.

'So considerate, my Daddy, but then you never would have bought me this stunning dress and put me in it knowing that you were gonna chastise me. So, you left your mark where none but us could see and where I'd be reminded, every time I sat down of our Rules. Our rules for living together, you cunt.' She quickly added, 'Fuck it, I can't remember when I started acting so girlishly again. Fuck it, it's just while he's not here, and as soon as he punishes me, Crystal will be back.

Because we're gonna live together, aren't we, huh? You want me to be your princess, and I knew, ha-ha, of course, I'd never say it to you for fear of more punishment, oh ouch! But I knew the first time our eyes met that you were lost in me.'

The voice sniggered again. *Fuck, I never enjoyed myself so much! What an absolute cunt you are!*

She turned quickly and violently towards it. 'Fuck you insignificant little twat.' and stroked her body in the claret, red and clingy dress.

The roundness of her full breasts was showcased perfectly; her slim legs drew the eye up to the micro-mini hem and made the mind wander.

Excitedly she stepped into the red spikes, so high that they perched her forward, making her breasts spill out tantalisingly. She twirled herself around, smiling wickedly at what she saw. 'Oh Daddy, you have no idea, you think you planned this? I knew the first time I saw you that I would possess you.' She giggled nervously and pressed her finger to her lips. 'Shh baby girl.'

She squealed and went to find her phone.

'Damn it, ugh yeah, you gave it to that guy when I was in our limo! And there's me not even thinking of it until now! Until I gotta see the time. Fuck you would roar at this, Daddy, coz I live on it, but not since this since meeting you.'

She looked around for a clock.

It's 6.50 the voice said and disappeared. She knew it wouldn't be back until she was on her own again,

'Thanks, cunt,' she muttered and ran to the lift just in

time, as she stepped into the foyer, the old guy on reception drew in a short breath.

'Oh, you can look all you want, you disgusting little creep,' she said viciously over her shoulder and stepped into the crisp winter sunshine.

The beautiful silver ghost limo shone in its light, and she hesitated before the door. It was opened, and a well-manicured hand beckoned her in. 'Come to Daddy, sweet cheeks. My oh my, you do polish up well.'

She blushed as he pulled her in, hesitating to think it was a little romantic and blushed again.

'Nearly?' he said.

'Nearly?' she replied.

'You nearly did that god-awful sniggering thing again now come here and let me inspect you.' Forcefully he dragged her onto his lap. 'Drive then, I don't expect to wait while you curtain twitches!' he said to the driver who had been eyeing her too long and had forgotten himself.

She enjoyed his possessive manner towards her and giggled and wriggled on his lap loving the heat from his swollen cock through his trousers.

'Daddy,' she whispered in his ear. 'I've never had such a good time, and neither will you.'

His hands slid up her body, rubbing her breasts and pushing her hard down on him. 'Oh you have no idea Baby girl, and yes you are right, I do think you're quite exceptional.'

She gasped, her breath went cold as ice as he ran his fingers across her throat,

'Now, get off and sit over there someplace, or we will never get to where we are going.'

His charm offensive was delicious. Nobody had ever spoken to her like it before, and she obeyed, sitting to the side and resting her hands between her slender legs.

'I can't help but wonder where you are taking me?' she said breathlessly, her nerves making her skin bristle and the pit of her stomach flutter.

'Patience, Baby girl, hasn't Daddy told you about this before? Will be so much more satisfying for the look on your face at every stage.'

'Oh,' she remarked, disappointed to see that they pulled up outside The Collared Kitten.

'You're disappointed? My case in point, the look on your face at this moment is priceless. Rest assured, little kitty kat, it will be an experience, and I really must just check-in, then Daddy has a treat for you, you will see.'

The stocky chauffeur opened the door, and they entered the club ushered in by two incredibly stunning but strong-looking female devils.

'Welcome to Hell,' one whispered to her as she passed, and a shiver went down her spine.

Robert Alexander took her arm softly, leading her through the luxurious and opulent corridor, the door was opened by Sadie who spoke excitedly to him,

'Did I do well, Sir?' She eyed his acquisition lustfully.

'Excellence is prevalent in you, my girl, and yes, she does look rather gratifying, doesn't she?'

He carried on through the club without pomp or ceremony. He wasn't the type to require it; he was stealth-like, panther-like, and nothing more needed to be said or done to announce his arrival.

Pure class, she thought, as he moved her into his private booth that was dark and only lit by red-shaded lamps, the leather on the chairs was luxurious and sumptuous. She sat next to him, attempting to snuggle up and whisper girlish charms, he got up and took her hands, she blushed as it felt tender.

'No baby girl, you get me all wrong, I don't want you sickly and clingy, and romance does not affect me. Surely you have gathered that already? Are you taking something?'

He yanked her to her feet. 'Once more baby girl, are you on something? Because that would just ruin the surprise, I have in store for you.' His grip was tight, and she held her breath, terrified to answer him, but she knew she must.

'No Daddy, honest I swear, I've never been into drugs, not even pot. Please let go of me you're hurting my arm.'

His grip softened and caressed where he had left a mark with his nails, his mouth was so soft and made her whole-body ache as his tongue travelled up her arm.

'I'm such a bad Daddy, am I not?' He directed her to sit opposite him.

'Here is where I want my princess to sit so as Daddy can watch her as she becomes aroused.'

She fell backwards into the soft, supple leather, not wanting to take her gaze from him. 'No Daddy, it's me that's bad, I shouldn't have presumed.' Her lips trembled, and tears filled her eyes, but she held them from falling, she knew that his comment was meant to have that effect and she knew she had to take full blame for him becoming aggressive toward her. She had made him lose composure and now knew that at some point, she would pay for that.

Yet again, she sat before him nervous and unsure what to do. His stare penetrated her soul, and she fidgeted with her clothes.

'Stop that, it's so annoying, baby girl.'

She placed her hands between her thighs as his stare ventured there, and she knew what he wanted. She knew he wanted to play,

The curtains opened as her hands slid in her knickers, and she blushed as the waiter entered, 'Your champagne, Sir, and is it the same for the lady?'

Robert Alexander stifled a laugh. 'But I do not see, nor do I want a lady. Crystal, what's your tipple?'

She took a deep breath and sat forward pensively, knowing that each word he said was a test, each question a riddle,.'I quite like JD 'n' Coke,' she whispered nervously.

He shared a look with the waiter.

'Champagne it is then, Sir,' the waiter said and placed the flute before her, leaving her with the hardest look she felt she'd ever seen.

Robert Alexander toyed with his glass rimming the edge till it began to hum in her ears, she obsessively watched him.

'Do help yourself. You'll wait a very long time if you want me to pour for you.'

He helped himself to some of the bubbly and pushed the bottle towards her.

Her mouth grimaced at his assault, how could he at one point be so charming and in the blink of an eye so cutting.

'But you enjoy it, Babygirl,' he said cryptically, answering her thoughts. 'I do so enjoy the cut and thrust of the flow of your emotions - it's quite hot and sexy.'

She blushed and stifled a giggle, grabbed the bottle, and overfilled her glass nervously. It flowed out of the top and onto the table.

'I'm sorry!' She grabbed a napkin and started mopping it up, 'I'm such a clumsy person, Mr, truly I am I think I began to tell you.'

'Crystal, save me the details. It's not that I'm in any rush just that I'm not interested in character flaws and bear with me girl before you burst into floods of tears.'

She trembled, trying not to cry.

'I do find you physically very appealing; also, there is a sweet innocence about you. You, for all your wild ways and manners, will never be anything other than a vulnerable mess; always so eager to believe, no matter how many times you have been hurt.'

He sat forward in his chair and stretched out his arm, pushing her thighs gently apart, 'If you pleased, Daddy, you would feel so much better, all that emotion needs a sweet release.' His touch was soft, but his manner was firm. She knew what he wanted and hated that it made her so hot.

Stupid slut, why are you acting coy? It's so fucking ugly like you haven't done worse, the vicious voice whispered. *'Now you gonna snigger, and he hated that.'*

She took a deep breath, trying not to but sniggered all the same. 'I'm sorry Daddy, I'm just nervous. I know that looks ugly.'

He loosened his tie and looked her in the eye. 'It's not the most prominent thing on my mind.'

Blushing, she shifted around in her seat, knowing he wanted her to start. Her fingers slipped to her wet panties then up to her aroused nipples she kneeled on the chair opening her legs and began to writhe under her touch and his stare, her hand slipped to her throat and hair. She groaned as she caressed her wet pussy.

'Daddy touch me please,' she sighed as her clit slipped between her fingers. She arched back and felt his hand grip her throat - his thumb stroking her until she began to pant.

He took off his belt and unzipped his trousers, forcing her back, his mouth grazed hers as he pushed himself in her hard, grabbing her hair and forcing her to arch backward. His hard cock pounded her; his breath was hot on her throat as his teeth sunk in, and she moaned in agony and ecstasy as his juice filled her, hot cum oozing into her wanting body.

'I'd love to have your baby,' she cried out, immediately regretting it as he let out a throaty laugh.

'Oh wow, Baby girl, not exactly what I expected... He held his finger to her lips. '... but then that's why I chose you, for moments like this.'

He pulled out of her and closed her legs, pulling down her dress. 'Now then, sit by Daddy. You have been such a good girl, and I want you to see through my eyes those that frequent this type of club. It's not to judge just to show you why I found you so attractive, hmm? For it's a sure thing though you're pretty there are others far more favoured, but you have something they don't. I want you to try to forget your inhibitions and tell Daddy why he chose you, show Daddy, but that part I'll savour later.'

One of his devil girl bodyguards pulled back the curtain, and The Collared Kitten's vibe and pulse began to throb around her body.

She felt his finger touch hers, and with the other hand, he pointed out scenes and people asking her what she thought, what she saw.

At first, she found it difficult, but then under his direction began to analyse the scene.

He was pleased with her, stroking her cheek and hair, and the more she gave, the more she enjoyed his attention.

Stupid cunt, the vicious voice sniped in her ear. *He's analysing you not enjoying your perspective, Sherlock.* It laughed bitterly in her ear and made her blush and forget herself for a moment, but Daddy was not having that,

'Oh dear, that damned voice, still Daddy has you now and to be honest I do so enjoy your Madonna type appearance. The fact that you are tortured is incredibly erotic to me, do you think that's wrong, baby girl? For Daddy to find your vulnerability attractive?' He pulled her face towards him tracing his tongue across her lips.

She clasped her hands in her lap, nervously. 'I've

been told that it shouldn't be so, that my disability should never be found attractive, but...'

'Shh, Daddy knows, for you see all those quacks have made you feel so ugly because your impairment is as integral to you as the colour of your eyes. I'm right, aren't I? So, you see, to me, it is quite divine. I get so bored with normal girls. I never had one beyond making them lose it, a different type of pleasure I enjoy in arid times.'

She was lost in his eloquent words, and though no scholar she did enjoy, found attractive, a well-educated gentleman. However, up until now, they hadn't enjoyed her.

'Now princess, I want my tiny tiger to show me more, going to let you explore, but first I want you to see this. 'He pressed a button concealed in the arm of the sumptuous chair which revealed close circuit tv.

'Off with you then, Daddy will be watching.'

Nervously she stood up, her legs shaking as his hand slid between her thighs and caressed her wet lips.

He tapped her ass, and she took a deep breath, joining the party that was playing on the screen.

CHAPTER 10

She stroked a table where two men sat and fingered the glasses, utterly unaware of her actions.

One of the many beautiful female security intervened as one of the men went to grab her. 'Oh honey, she's not for you, this little one is special if you know what I mean?'

He was drunk, they both were, and he laughed, slumped in his chair. 'Oh, but see I kind of like her and am only interested in special.' He went to grab her ass again, but the female twisted his arms behind his back and forced his face onto the table. His friend jumped up and went to swing for her as she ground his face into the glass that had broken, another guard kicked the friend in the nuts from behind, and he fell to the floor crying.

They dragged them both to their feet and marched them out as Sadie sauntered over, taking Crystal by the waist with a feather-like touch and moving her through the club. 'A little detour and the first of your surprises.'

She winked at her as she pulled her through the club scene to the stage. Crystal had wondered wide-eyed at this the night before and the intense erotic dancers that frequented it.

She gasped, 'Am I gonna dance here?'

Sadie took her to the side of the stage to the steps. 'Well, of course, honey bunny, every special kitten gets the last dance.'

Crystal's heartbeat out of her chest, her mouth so full it became dry again, and she cursed the voice that sniggered at it saying her teeth were stuck to her lips.

She wet them. 'Last? Oh, hell yeah, I see, because Daddy wouldn't want me parading anything after we are firmly together. I wanted this so bad Sadie but was too nervous just to join in last night.'

Sadie laughed to herself, and it stung a bit as Crystal could see it was sarcasm. 'I guess you're laughing because you never really come across someone like me, huh? Or that your Daddy is soon gonna have a proper old school girlfriend? Ha, I say girlfriend, but I'd be more like a mistress; he is pleased with me,' she added bitterly through gritted teeth.

Sadie pulled her to sit on the stage steps. 'Oh baby, we are all so happy with you.' She was still laughing, but her words and manner calmed crystal. 'And yeah, this stage is for you. I have a couple of nobodies to help you out, you see?'

She gestured to the stage where two divine creatures were dancing together within an occult circle, rubbing and daubing red paint over each other. They methodically licked each other as they traced sabres across their bodies, pretending to wound. Each strike was followed by touching and screeching as if they feasted off each other.

Crystal bit her lip. 'I don't see a couple of nobodies.'

Sadie pulled her to her feet and onto the stage. 'Appearances aren't everything honey, and neither of these two has ever been chosen. Damn it. I have a knack for stating the obvious.'

Crystal laughed and felt empowered by her words.

'Gonna leave you to em now, Sweets.'

She was gone before Crystal could turn around from the erotic dancing display.

Nervously she stood there, not quite sure what she should do. Both girls eyed her and screamed in high pitched unison. Crystal shook, watching them approach her as they snaked and grinder the floor with each step and rolling hip.

'Hi,' she said, then cursed herself for sounding like an idiot.

Neither answered, but both took her arms and, with red leather, whips bound her to their waists. They moved back to centre stage and Crystal, feeling intensely aroused.

She was between them as they began to dance sensuously around her, her hands instinctively worked their exposed erotic zones. She felt alive, like every nerve in her body was being stroked by the devil.

One quickly drew her sabre while the other grabbed her by the throat and pulled her head back as it was traced along the line from ear to ear and neck. She screamed, she knew they wouldn't kill her, but they could slip, and she hated herself for shouting, 'No!'

They ignored her and carried on, the sabre being guided across every erogenous zone there was until she was begging for them to go deeper, harder. She gasped, her hips grinding the girl behind her and her hands tangled in her hair.

The girl backed off, one licking her lips, both screamed again as though it was what they wanted. One came from behind Crystal and, with her sabre, sliced through the whips. They ran to each other in ecstasy, kissing passionately then bowing to her as they left the stage.

She was breathless excited and darkly intoxicated, so aroused, but not only by the girls. She loved that she had all eyes on the display they had been cumming hard, she'd seen punters jerking off, eyes fixed on them, and now they wouldn't leave her. Unfortunately, now it made her stressed and as she started to run.

Sadie appeared, saying, 'Oh baby, that was divine. Now come with me, Sugar Tits, I have another little detour then the second of your surprises. Got some old faces you might wanna see and maybe you could dance for us again?'

Where Robert Alexander parted the crowds with an ominous presence, Sadie flirted her way through and was popularity itself. People joked and winked and tapped her cheeky ass, which she always replied to with some smart quip or equally sharp sexual harassment.

Crystal was in awe of her confidence, though when she tried to copy her, it was awkward, and she quickly decided to leave it to Sadie and let her guide her.

She was scared even to think that she found her a turn on, weirdly she thought Daddy knew all her thoughts, and after all, he had organised Her last dance, which was so fucking hot. Anger bubbled up in her, I kind of hope, no, I know you're jealous over me,

Daddy, that was a test of your dominance over me, and I'd say I passed. Yeah, that's it, you just love the control and fuck it, so do I.

She blushed heavily as she spotted one of the cameras.

'Oh, Honey, he likes it. This is your special night. You wanna touch, Sadie?'

She stopped at a booth and traced a finger across Crystal's face, softly taking her hand, sliding it up her waist and to her soft curvaceous breasts. She smiled gently, letting her hand drift down to her thighs. 'Wanna feel more? I am kinda sweet on you.'

Crystal felt the heat between her legs, gliding her finger to Sadie's wet lips and dipped in, stroking her clit. Sadie's eyes burned with passion. 'Your touch is divine, no wonder he wants you so bad, and I've been a bit naughty tasting his supper, but as I'm a favourite. I'm sure he'll let me off. I say let me off, but then he never got on, something you got that I ain't. As he says, 'It ain't something for you to yearn for... that would be weird.' No, it's something for him too.'

She giggled wickedly, her softness fleetingly leaving

her face to look demonic, her eyes blackening even further, a harshness flickered across it.

'Oops, nearly forgot myself,' she said as her gentle expression returned. 'Come on then, Babe, let's have some fun, and I'll have the honour of delivering your first surprise tonight.'

She pulled her to the dance floor. 'So how are you finding our special host?' she quizzed as they made their way through the dancers, Sadie, all the while flirting dangerously with all. Crystal thought that if she ever tried it, she would be raped, at least where she came from.

Southampton was a backwater compared to Soho, and the Hampshire men still bore the ignorance and chauvinistic attitude of their grandfathers.

'You don't need to answer that baby. There ain't one girl he chose yet that has come back to complain if you know what I mean?' The last part was lost on Crystal. 'I think he's all that, at least I think he's a very private man?'

Sadie smiled, acknowledging it. 'Uh-huh, you see those two over there? Remember them?' The two girls she had danced with previously were vying for top spot Crystal immediately noticed how they performed in front of the cameras.

She shuddered at the black rage she felt.

Fucking sluts, no fucking chance.

'Oh, now honey, that doesn't suit you. Such a sour expression?' Sadie pinched her ass. 'Sure they're pretty, but they ain't you, Precious. Wanna ruin their night?'

Crystal's eyes grew wide as she hungered for more.

'Let them know who you are with, sad fucking squaws.' She pushed her forward and winked, leaving her and disappearing into the throbbing crowd.

One of them, the dark girl who had found Crystal so appealing before, waved excitedly over to her, the blonde snatched her hand down. It dragged her by the hair to the side where she shouted at her, trying not to look conspicuous. Her words were lost in the music, but Crystal knew exactly what they were or would be and lapped up every syllable.

She moved sensuously towards them, sliding in between. 'Wanna drink?' she shouted to the dark girl as she rubbed up to her, her hands sliding down her back and across her waist.

The dark girl nodded and took her hand, and the blonde's leading them to the bar.

The Scandinavian looking siren was furious, and it showed, but she joined them despite it. Crystal saw how she was calculating and tasted her blood, knowing she was just about to deal her a vicious blow, 'Oh shit girls!' she shouted, 'I don't have any money!'

The blonde laughed and was about to reply, but Crystal couldn't wait any longer,

'You see, I'm hooked up with a Robert Alexander? Do you know him? Just he has all these rules and surprises and stuff, and I gotta virtually forget who I am!'

The girl's looked shocked, the blonde in particular, and as the dark one went to speak, her mouth trembling and face drawn the blonde slapped her. 'Shut your fucking mouth before it ruins everything, ok?'

'Oh ouch, hey, no need to be mean.' Crystal cuddled the dark girl and smiled triumphantly at the blonde. 'So as I said, I got no money, just he took all my possessions off me and now I'm like his' property,' huh, weird but cool yeah?'

'Hey girl, you enjoy that for as long as you can't say I'm jealous though you seem to think I am.' the blonde started laughing and fell back onto the dark one.

Crystal was enraged. 'He's my fucking Daddy, ok? You cheap fucking whore!'

She grabbed her by the throat and squeezed it, the girl started to choke. Her friend l tried to pull Crystal's hands away.

'Hey, it's ok, we know he's yours, don't we?' she pointedly said to the blonde who nodded as best she could as Crystal's fingers tightened.

She let her hand slip down her neck and ran a finger across her jugular, 'Sadie? His favourite? She called you squaws, so funny, and we are so close. I might go looking for her again coz I have done what she told me to do and showed you up for the cheap jealous slags you are.'

The blonde sobbed and was shaken. 'We gonna go now, ok?' She was trembling as Crystal still had her pinned.

'Oh, sure, ha! I forget myself; you toddle off now. Find somewhere more suitable or even somewhere you have a chance of getting lucky but don't come back here, ok?'

She smiled smugly to herself as she saw them shakily

move away. A tap on her shoulder made her swing around aggressively, instinctively at the thought she was in trouble. So many times in clubs, she had been in scrapes and ejected aggressively. Her hands were up, ready to lash out when she saw Sadie standing there, laughing.

'Girl, that was something to see!' She embraced her and led her to a seat, 'Come on Baby, calm down now, I feel kinda guilty as I set you up there. I know a fighter from across the street on a moonless night with no street-lamps.' She pulled Crystal's hair back and planted a soft kiss on her nose.

'Ugh god, I feel like an idiot! Did many people see?'

Sadie laughed again. 'I'm quite sure you made a few freaks night with it, so don't fret honey. Ah, but I see you still do,' she looked at her with a fake grumpy face. 'Now didn't I say I had a surprise for you from your extraordinary gentleman?'

She took her fingertips and pulled her up. 'Come with me, he sure does think highly of you to have laid on such a treat!'

Crystal felt butterflies invade her stomach and excitedly blushed. 'Show me, oh wow, he does like me, ya know I knew he did, and I was trying to make him see but seems I didn't have to.'

Sadie blushed too but not in the same way. 'Baby, there's been many before you, and there will be plenty after, just enjoy the ride, ok honey?'

Crystal winced a little, but as was her way and she quickly shrugged it off thinking bitterly for the first time about Sadie.

You just think he's all yours you sado. I see no ring on your finger or him treating you as anything other than a pimp.

She hid her thoughts well, she had always believed that and had never been found out until she stopped, for sure.

Daddy would know them.

Her head swung around, looking for signs of him or cameras. Still, Sadie was intent on dragging her to wherever and it irritated. That said, it also didn't allow her to feel that sickening paranoia the quacks had told her about.

She found herself at a small dark door, almost cave-like.

'Cute, huh?' Sadie said, as she entered a code and it swung open. 'You just wait for a second, I almost forgot.' She took a black blindfold out of her top and turned Crystal around, 'to increase the pleasure, honey.' She tied it softly and stroked her neck to reassure her. 'Such a nervous Kitten you, I think that's why you're so special to him.'

She guided her forward, and Crystal heard the door close softly behind them.

'I'm so excited. I gotta show you!' Sadie whipped the blindfold off and gestured to the fantastic entertainment Robert Alexander had put on.

Crystal's adrenaline was pumping violently as she took it all in, Alice?'

'Uh-huh, ain't it something to see? And all for you, sweetness! Now I gotta leave you as he wants just you captured, not boring old me, ain't that what you thought back there? You got a little bit distressed. I see a lot in faces, little one.'

Before Crystal could wipe the shock from her face or cover up what she had thought, Sadie disappeared, locking the door behind her.

She eyed all that was before her, forgetting Sadie's observation quickly. 'Oh Daddy, oh shit, I forgot you're watching and probably listening. Shit, there I go again with the disrespect! Ha, I was gonna say how special I feel, but your pimp saw to that, so I won't bother, fuck it. Why can't I shut my mouth and just enjoy this? Hell, I will coz I don't believe I'm nothing to you. I do know some stuff about human beings, and I know when a guy is smitten…'

She stopped herself mid-sentence, feeling embarrassed and humiliated. 'But hey, this is the most exciting thing that ever happened to me, so I'm gonna enjoy it!'

She ran her finger across a table, simply adorned with two treats, one saying, DRINK ME, the other saying, EAT ME.

'Should I? I mean it's kinda scary but then so am I sometimes, oh fuck it I'm just gonna down it ha, can't be much in it, right? No need to drug me or nothing.'

Her hands were shaking as she picked up the small bottle and held it to her trembling lips. It smelled of aniseed, and within seconds she was licking her lips and trying to get more from the bottle.

'I guess this is gonna be just as sweet?' she said as she picked up the small tray of caviar and oysters. 'I never tried em, but I reckon you must think I'm worth it so here goes.' She held her nose and swallowed an oyster, quickly spooning in the caviar with the tiny spoon.

'Oh wow, that was lush!' she said, licking her lips. 'I was always told oysters were like snot and caviar, but let's not go there!'

She took a deep breath and made her way to the sumptuous couch and sat down, putting her feet up.

'Ha, I feel kinda sleepy, maybe I'll take a nap? Hey, Daddy if that was drugged, I won't know the difference - you have no idea how screwed up I am, ain't that right you sick mother fucker?'

She gestured wildly, listening for the voice but was beginning to feel dizzy. 'That's my psycho friend I'm talking to, D.' The words escaped her; her brain unable to engage. So, she laughed again, slumping in the chair.

'Just a little nap, wow I'm already dreaming this is so cool.' her words were slurred as her head fell onto her chest. Dizzily she raised it as the door creaked open and Sadie and two others appeared. 'Ha, err fuck, am I home? And that's, fuck, who are you?'

Sadie grabbed her hair back and whispered in her ear. 'Shut your fucking filthy mouth you low life tramp and do as your told or this is the end of the road for you, sweetness. '

Crystal was dribbling, and Sadie looked at her disgusted, then licked it. 'Just wanna taste for me too.'

She was propped up between the other two, and Sadie led the way. 'Just another silly country girl who did too much candy!' she laughed, as Crystal was dragged through the crowd. 'Why he insists on this dramatic flair is beyond me,' she shouted to Crystal over the music and lifted her chin.

'There's a back way outta that place, but he seems to enjoy this bit!'

She let her jaw drop as they exited the central part of the club. Crystal's feet scuffed and dragged along the carpet, and as they hit the fresh night air, Sadie commanded that they lift her.

She was pushed onto the back seat of a limo, and Sadie aggressively threw her legs in, 'So Long sweet cheeks, it's been wild, enjoy your trip.' She slammed the door, and the car pulled off slowly. Crystal was trying to mouth words to the driver, who put his screen up viciously. She banged on the window. She thought she did; she thought she shouted for help.

'Daddy! Where are you?'

The driver answered. 'Oh poor wee baby, not long now and you'll be seeing him again, you poor stupid fuck.'

'Huh? Oh, I'm going to, Da…' she slumped again as the car rolled and leaned her face against the cold glass of the window to try to sober up.

THEY PULLED UP AT THE APARTMENTS, AND SHE WAS pulled from within the limo hurriedly and quietly. Someone had their hand over her mouth, and shouted, 'God she's sick again!'

She was dragged through the foyer, and when she started to laugh was slapped by someone which made her laugh harder, then she was thrown into the lift on her own as it ascended to the penthouse, it felt slower this time.

She managed to stand and try to check herself out in the mirror, her make-up was streaked, and she sobbed and hit the glass as the door pinged and darkness tinged with candlelight flooded in.

The lift light went out.

CHAPTER 11

'Mister? Daddy? She cried as she fumbled to get out of the lift, the doors opening and closing rapidly.

The light was so low, and she thought she could see something lit on the floor, some sort of drawing.

'Well, well, kitty cat, a bit of a mess, aren't you? Still, that's to be expected.'

She could hear his voice came from the couch and strained to see his dark figure in the shadows. She listened to his footsteps coming towards her. 'Daddy, I'm sorry I think someone slipped me something?'

'Oh yes, that would be me,' he said as he grabbed her by the hair and pulled her out of the lift. 'Daddy wants Tuppence, you see? A little dark magic and Crystal loses her grip on that precious little fuck up.'

She let out a high-pitched scream as he yanked her to the floor, 'Oh hush now, Tuppence, this is what you wanted, isn't it?'

She could make out the drawing now; it was a pentagram with each point lit with a tiny candle.

'Please, Daddy, I don't understand?' She fumbled within the occult symbol sobbing and pulling her knees up to her chest. 'Tuppence is nobody!' she growled, his hand went to her throat and stroked it firmly with his thumb.

'But Tuppence is all I wanted, baby girl. Crystal is so shallow and fake and has nothing to offer me. She's not real.'

He pulled her thighs apart, and his head dipped lower. 'This is too precious for a two-bit whore called Crystal, and Daddy must punish that Crystal, hmm? For being so mean and stealing her away from me.'

She could see his huge hard cock in the light: he was naked with strange drawings all over his body. He pinned her aggressively, his thighs so hard and muscular, his grip tightening on her throat to the point she began to feel herself stop breathing.

He released, then gripped again.

He forced himself hard into her aching body. 'Tuppence,' he whispered hotly in her ear as he moved roughly on her, her pussy crying out for more.

'Yes, Daddy,' she replied, loving his grind so bad that she tore at his back with her nails, feeling the flesh open beneath them.

Her thighs wrapped around his hot torso, wanting it harder and faster, his sweat making her nipples ache as his chest brushed hers with every stroke.

She caught the fierce look on his face, and it took her breath away.

'So much anger from you, Tuppence, Daddy likes it.'

He pulled out his hot cock, flipped her over, circling

her ass with it, and covered in her juices. He entered her so quickly, she fell forward, and his hand grabbed her neck, pinning her face down as he pounded her.

He rode her ass until she was screaming out and cumming hard, sliding his cock from her tight gripping buttocks, flipping her onto her back and driving his cock deep.

'Fuck me harder, Daddy!' she screamed out primitively, tearing at his back and gasping as she felt he was about to ejaculate.

He arched back, his magnificent body too much for her to take as she clawed at his chest, feeling his juice fill her, and his body shudder in pleasure.

He slid out of her wet cunt and back on his haunches, his eyes on fire, his breathing rasping and hard, his cock dripping, hard and twitching.

A circle of blood-soaked sand surrounded the pentagram. She fingered it as she rolled her head wildly, her throat so orgasmic it was driving her mad.

'When will it stop, Daddy?' she moaned, terrified to touch it in case she passed out. He traced his finger from ear to ear and down her jugular.

'Daddy will look after his princess, you will see. Now that, that whore Crystal is gone.'

His hand hovered over her heart, which raced and boomed as he circled it with his finger.

He pulled her to her feet then beckoned she follow him to the bed, even darker. She could barely make anything out, so she stretched out her hands, looking for him.

'Here, he said, guiding her with his voice until her

hands touched the bed. She gasped when she felt his body so close, the drugs, shock, fear, and excitement, making her pee herself slightly.

'Oh Daddy, I'm sorry.'

'Don't be, you are incredibly rewarding,' he said as his hand dipped between her thighs.

'But I'll make such a mess.'

She felt humiliated, and her legs were trembling.

'So, I can see you better,' he said as he lit a light which let out haunting shadows of objects she couldn't make out, the room seemed fuller and he was studying her face.

'More surprises for, Tuppence.' He pulled her closer to him until she could hear and feel his breath on her.

His juice was leaking from her pussy, running down and across her sore, harshly fucked ass.

Down her burning, punished cheeks, soaking the bedding. She looked down, shocked at his throbbing weapon, it was still hard and glistening from the mix of their cum.

As she looked at his face, she saw controlled lust. 'Please, Daddy, let me rest a short time, please?' she panted, as she covered her swollen wet pussy with her hand feeling the heat radiating from deep inside her body.

He reached down, removing her hand so he could see it. A smile flicked across his face as he told her firmly, 'One more, baby girl. One more kink before I let your body rest and cool. This will be something special, princess.'

He put her wet hand on his firm penis, wrapping it

around his girth, wanking himself with her hand. 'No one will ever do to you what I will, Tuppence.'

He knew she would give herself to him. Still, he waited to hear her words.

'Ok, Daddy, fuck me however you want, fuck me till I die.'

She laughed nervously but loved the fear and anticipation. Strangely, she felt as if he was unknown, that she was just meeting him for the first time. She wanted to run but couldn't, her passion for him overriding any instinct she began to feel.

'You know I would do anything for you.'

'Good girl.' He lent into her and kissed her deeply, his tongue delving in her mouth and his hand holding and supporting the back of her neck, keeping her tight to him. Her hand still around his cock, he took her hair with both hands, tilting her head back and looking her in the eyes.

'Now lick Daddy clean. Lick my cock and balls until I tell you enough, and then I want you to suck Daddy's cock harder than you have before. You're going to ask me to fuck your face, do you understand, Tuppence?'

She felt the rage that she had once before because he kept calling her that stupid bitch name, Tuppence. But she was not giving up now. *You owe me so much, fuck me as much as you want, but I'm going to get your wallet and bleed you dry, you fucker.*

'Do you understand?' he said, shaking her by the hair.

'Yes, Daddy, fuck me, use me for your pleasure please.'

Her mind was made up, her body cumming hard and her thighs hot, emotions between rage, obsession, and lust.

The smile that whipped across his face was not one she had seen before and sent icy cold instinctive fear through her. She hated herself for visibly shaking in response to it and bit her lip so hard that blood oozed out, he licked it off which made her want to grab him and hump him, grinding his hot cock. She pulled on it, ready to follow her instructions but was unable as he was still holding her head back.

He moved his mouth to her ear and whispered, 'Poor little Princess, wanting it so bad she would sell her soul.'

He got up, leaving her in the dim light. She watched his dark panther-like form retrieve something from the closet, he brought it back, buckled belt, stroking her with it and teasing her nipples and throat.

'A little binding to stop you lashing out and hurting Daddy with those sharp talons, hmm, Tuppence?'

'The belt?' she gasped.

'Oh no, that's for inflicting sweet agonies and punishing strikes on your cherry ass. Indeed, I have some restrictive ties for you, bearing in mind the more you struggle, the tighter they get.'

Her eyes popped as did her ears as she heard him grab something from the table. 'It's still so dark, Daddy. Can we have a little more light? I'd feel less nervous if I could see what was happening.'

'Light? Less nervous? But sweetheart, I like you nervous, there will be plenty of light at the end of your punishment when you have more clarity of thought than you ever dreamed possible.'

She pulled her knees up in a defensive position again, his soft firm grip parted them and pulled them down. 'No need baby girl, would Daddy ever do anything you didn't crave? Do you remember a little conversation you had with Sadie?'

Her mouth and throat were dry, with the adrenaline pumping round her body. Her heart thumped rapidly as all she could think of was the pleasure he was giving her.

Even if it hurts a bit, I kinda like it, she whispered in her mind, hoping, longing to hear the strangely reassuring bitterness of the voice.

I *rewarded her with a snigger.*

'Oh, your threshold for pain and pleasure is gonna be tested now, you sad fucking whore.'

She blushed and could feel her cheeks burn in contrast to the ice that was pumping through her veins; her breath was so cold and dry.

Robert Alexander pushed her face down onto the sheets and, in one movement, took both her arms and bound them with something scratchy, which felt like plastic. His hands then moved to her legs, running his hands up to them, her thighs parted as she breathed huskily with fear and anticipation. She felt him stretch them to their limits then bind them to the bed.

'I'm not going to gag you, baby girl, not yet anyway.' His fingers stroked her rosebud lips. 'I want to hear every cry and whimper, and every time you beg me to stop, I will become harsher. Your body and mind are too weak to cope with pleasure; you will beg.'

Tears rolled down her cheeks; the atmosphere was so potent and electric, fuelled with passion and eroticism, and she dared to think that she had never felt so alive.

'And so close to death,' he answered.

'Death?' she replied, her lips trembling as the word escaped her.

'Oh, but you see, that is where the gods like to fuck and straddle the line between life and death continuously. Pray then little one that you have a goddess residing in you.'

She giggled nervously as she felt his weight behind her, grabbing her hair. He entered her aggressively, biting down hard on the back of her neck until she screamed out in agony and ecstasy.

His pounding was so fast and hard that she began to gag, 'Daddy, my ass can't take it, please Daddy?' He drove harder in her with each cry keeping his promise, his harsh words screwing with her mind as she wanted them to, wanted so as he would make her feel better later.

He pulled out as she felt his cock twitching and about to cum. 'This is going to be so sweet; I need to savour every moment.'

She twisted her neck to see him move in the dark shadows, taking something from the table again.

'Good girl,' he said, as he came behind her. 'Such a good girl and so deserving of special treatment.' She felt cold steel trace a line down her spine, and she knew it was a knife and screamed as she felt him make tiny incisions with the knife tip down.

She was desperate to feel like a goddess; she wanted to please him and be everything to him.

'I love it, Daddy! I never thought cutting could feel so divine, am I a goddess now, Daddy?' She bit down hard on her lip again as the steel travel up to her neck to her jugular. She couldn't show fear now, it would ruin everything, but her body was trembling violently.

'Oh, you are truly such, so deliciously receptive and trusting. Your innocence is breath-taking.'

The knife toyed with her throat for what seemed like hours; she held her breath. He pulled the blade down her jugular firmly but not enough to cut her. He could see the terror within her by the shakes and twitches as he played with her.

'Now for the belt, the exquisite pain and pleasure is my pleasure to administer.'

She watched him put the knife on the bedside cabinet with exceptional care and pick up the coiled belt he had just mentioned. The voice returned. *We'll stick him with the knife, see how he likes it. Once he unties you, get it, you stupid fucking bitch!*

She watched as he allowed the belt to unroll, he was holding the buckle and began to wind the belt around his hand, that rich, thick leather sound seemed so loud to her. He moved to the side of the bed and studied Crystals form in the dim light, making her wait, knowing the anticipation would be driving her mad,

She bit the sheets hard as she felt the first strike, the pain shocked her but the throbbing after made her want more, her ass cumming so hard it made her pussy ache. He stroked the buckle across her cheeks.

'More?' he whispered, 'beg me for more.'

She had to, she had no choice, and she truly believed this was everything she ever wanted, had missed out on, and she needed to be the goddess. Then the author of his most extreme fantasy, 'Please Daddy, gimme more,' she finally said as she heard the belt fly through the air, but this time it was the buckle that hit. Her scream of agony was spine chilling, high pitched, and desperate as she sobbed onto the sheets.

She felt the gash the belt had made and blood seeping on to her buttock.

'But you want it? Like it?' he said, inches from her face. 'Do you want to be my goddess or not, hmm?'

'Oh yes, Daddy, with all my heart. I didn't mean to scream,' she choked out, drowning in tears and feeling exalted in his eyes. 'I wanna be your goddess more than anything.'

'Very well,' he replied. 'But being a goddess, you shall certainly need slaves, girls to bathe and tend to you, hmm? I shall have to see what I can rustle up for my precious princess.'

Her shaking was intense, and she felt she was going to be sick.

'I love how you do that. It increases pleasure,' he said as he felt her legs trembling, leaning back and untying the leg binds, flipping her and sitting her up to face him, her arms still tightly tied behind her back. She loved how he maltreated her and shook as he positioned her for his next pleasurable torment.

'Daddy, I just need to ...to catch my breath.' He ignored her waving a candle before her and across her body.

'Ugh, my blood!' She was shocked to see it smeared over her thighs.

'Pretty isn't it?' he replied, moving the candle artistically over her form.

She was cold as ice and shaking uncontrollably. 'I never liked blood much before, Daddy, but I now think it is pretty as you say, no, I now see it as pretty for sure.'

The candle wax began to drip as he tilted it hitting her taut breasts and nipples, she held her breath so as not to react, feeling so hot as it hardened on them, I can't lose him now. I gotta be more to him, she thought, as he hoisted her knees and rocked her back, exposing her orgasmic pussy. He let the candle drip and catch her clit and her stressed lips, making her groan in pleasure as it dried and tightened on them. He showed her, wanted her to admire his hot angry cock.

'So pleasing,' he said as he stroked it, his other hand stroking the back of her neck. The next 30 minutes, he spent dripping wax around her body, letting it dry and crumble as he turned and twisted her body.

Orgasm followed orgasm; Crystal's body being treated to a pain that she was craving.

'Feels like I'm gonna die, it's so good,' she softly and breathlessly. 'But you know what Daddy? I'd go happy. I'm not scared, you know. I want the ultimate, I want it all.'

She was shaking in pain, pleasure, and fear and could barely breathe and was terrified and hungry for more at the same time. Either she couldn't or didn't want to escape; some sick fantasy made her want to take it as if he'd feel jealousy over how magnificent she was going to prove she could be.

Robert Alexander blew out the candle and looked her in the eyes. 'I am going to fuck you one more time Tuppence, your pussy can then rest. First, let me see to those binds, no need now as I have you exactly as I want you.'

His fingers disposed of them in an instant and he thumbed where they had cut in, she shrieked quietly as he applied too much pressure which he silenced with a finger to his lips.

Crystal felt relief. She wanted to sleep so badly, all his dominance and punishment had exhausted her, and she wanted the pain to stop. Still, her buttocks stung, and in the back of her mind, she knew her exhaustion and soreness overwhelmed the kinky pleasure she had felt, but she couldn't lose this battle, she had to be the most extreme.

'Thank you, Daddy, you are too much for me, I know, but hopefully, I'm not disappointing? I hope you enjoyed me, and I'll soon learn to keep up with you!'

Robert Alexander hushed her, placing his finger to her quivering lips while reaching inside the bedside cabinet bringing out a black rubber gag.

'Let us get a little serious, huh, Tuppence?' he said, as he lifted her head with one hand.

'Open your plentiful little mouth princess.' Crystal complied with the request and gagged as he slipped in a thick dildo in the shape of three balls into her mouth. It was connected to a rubber strap, which he began to fasten around her head. In a panic, she lashed out, catching his chest with her nails and cutting him.

His look froze on her, those dark, cold eyes had never looked colder and just filled her with an unbearable fear, making her wish she had never met him.

Her tongue was forced down by the gag dildo, but her mouth was full, and she had to bite down on it to ease her reflex. She stared as he wiped the blood from his chest, first licking it and then rubbing it across her left breast, pinching her nipple spitefully.

She tried to scream but was unable, which made the pain feel greater.

'That's the spirit, Tuppence, Daddy likes a fighter, as it means they still need him.' His words were cold and not the Dominant Daddy of earlier.

His eyes were dark in the limited light, and Crystal was petrified.

He reached into the cabinet again and brought out a handful of plastic electrical ties. 'Daddy's little girl needs a little extra control now, don't you think? You have disregarded my trust by lashing out at me, hmm? Time to tether those talons again.'

She just stared, too scared to move or even nod, shake her head.

Robert Alexander grabbed Crystal's wrists, locking a cable tie on each. He then used a third to link, the two roughly holding her arms above her head, fastening it to a bar within the bed's headrest. He got up and secured her ankle to the other end of the bed, splaying her legs wide apart.

Looking up at him, Crystal had never felt so out of control in a situation. The fear made her vomit bile into her mouth, turning her head to the side to allow it to leak from her.

He then ensured each cable tie was tight, tight enough that they dig deep into her flesh. Crystal bite down hard on her gag, reacting to the pain. She found that if she moved, they cut into her flesh so kept a still as possible, hardly daring to breathe as the pain intensified.

He looked at her in the eyes and smiled, pointing at the ceiling, letting her know she could watch what he was doing in the mirrors. Reaching for the knife on the cabinet, he showed it to her, rotating it, lapping up the terror in her eyes. He began to draw it over her skin, not cutting, just teasing her cheeks, running it gently down her sleek neck, pushing it against her jugular, but drawing no blood. The knife traced around her breasts, he grabbed a nipple roughly and drew the blade around it.

She gritted her teeth against the rubber bung in her mouth in anticipation of the pain to come. He released her nipple and continued his sick teasing of her body with the knife. She panted in relief when he left her nipples and tried to calm herself that this was yet another sick game of his, thinking, I will use that knife to cut your fucking dick!

It glided over her sore, sodden pussy and down her inner thigh. When it reached her feet, he dragged the blade over her sole. She twitched uncontrollably, which caused the ties to cut into her wrists and ankles.

'Was I cruel to you? I guess you want me to untie

you now? Ok, princess, that's a good lesson you have learned.'

He saw the relief in her eyes, the realisation that he was playing with her, and then the terror and pain as he slowly sliced open her thigh, her eyes popping out of her head. He drew the blade about half an inch deep, from her knee to her upper leg, enjoying the sight of the flesh parting and the muscle below being visible.

She tried to scream, unsure what had happened to cause her so much pain, but her mouth bung stopped her and made her head pound so painfully. Tears welled up in her eyes, blurring her vision.

Robert Alexander's smile looked horrific with controlled pleasure, not angry and not in any rush, but living her pain as sexual pleasure.

She saw with horror, the torn blurry reflection of her thigh sliced open, the wound full of blood, and as she quivered, it poured over the sides of the injury.

She watched as Robert Alexander ran his tongue along the wound, slurping her blood as he did, his tongue delved into her flesh as if he was kissing her.

He drew the blade along her other thigh, watching her body convulse in pain as he tongued this new wound and allowed his fingers to delve and play with the previous. He groaned in the same manner as when he had sex, moving up Crystal's body and hovering over her mouth.

He opened him, allowing her blood to dribble from his mouth into hers.

The blood splattered in her eyes and nose; she could

smell it and taste it as it ran down the gag into her mouth along with her tongue and then down her throat.

Every slice was making his eyes hotter with desire; every taste of her fresh leaking blood make his member twitch. He fingered her wounds, drawing close to cumming. He took pleasure watching her, getting off on her pain and terror, keeping her alive by avoiding significant arteries, smiling as the blood spread everywhere.

He drew the knife along her upper arms, splitting her beautiful soft flesh open, enjoying the visual of her blood pouring over her skin. He forced his face into each arm, feeding on her, tonguing her as if he was giving her oral sex.

He looked up to ensure Crystal was still watching, his face and body painted red with her life's blood, looking her in the eyes and sliding a finger into her arm as he plucked at the central nerve, laughing at her tortured face.

Her body twisted in unbearable agony, her wrists and ankles now also bleeding as the cable ties cut the flesh.

She was now cold, opening her eyes that were blurred with blood and tears, the mirror reflecting her body lying in pools of blood, her hair caked in it where he had grabbed and run his fingers through.

The pain and exhaustion she was feeling from the arduous torturous kinks made her begin to wonder if her fantasy was for her to die for him? She wanted blood wanted to cross the ultimate boundary.

She begged in her mind for the bastard to finish it, her rage welled up inside, wanting to spit in his face.

Who the fuck? She thought. As sophisticated as his assault had been, she still recognised a player when she met one.

Fucking idiot! You gave yourself willingly like a fucking sado!

She didn't even care if he could read those thoughts. She wouldn't scream for him to let her go or stop the pain, and she bristled with a twisted pride knowing the time was close for the final performance. Now and then, her eyes drifted to the ceiling mirrors.

It ain't fucking pretty you cunt, lemme tell you. You are shit at that.

So cold and thirsty, the fear had made her dry up, and her mind kept slipping into a semi-state of unconsciousness.

He was licking her open wounds, making her feel sick as his tongue delved deep into the cuts on her thighs and arms, smiling as he tasted her blood. She put it down to the pain, but it felt like his tongue was in her legs at the same time, she could see him running his tongue in the open flesh, horror filing every nerve ending that was exposed.

He forced his cock inside her again, her body so limp and exhausted that, with every thrust, she wanted to die. She had stopped cumming and turned her head to look at his fierce face. He was laughing and talking, but it was muffled like a drone.

Was he talking to her or himself? She didn't care anymore, she just wanted to get this over and the pain to subside.

Terror filled what was left of her. She gagged weakly, feeling the vomit fill her mouth but had no energy to do it, so let it dribble out. As she closed her eyes, he slapped her face, roughly saying, 'I don't want you to miss anything.' She looked terrified, as over his shoulders appeared the two girls from the club, Elizabeth and Georgia. They were behind him, kissing each other with blood-soaked faces.

She knew then, vomiting again, that they had been licking at her wounds with him.

You cunt, you fucking sad cunt. So, fucking inadequate that you needed back up. Read that you miserable cunt!

They had shared her while he had been fucking her and was not some dull memory or pathetic fear. They had played her too, and her mind spun with grief and humiliation. It hurt as much as the cuts and the aggressive fucking. As they kissed each other Crystal's blood dripped from their mouths and onto his back, she glanced back at him as he sat up and passionately kissed them both, licking blood from their faces and still pounding Crystal's tired body.

He drew the knife over her stomach and breasts, not cutting but tracing lines, paying her no attention apart from the brutal fucking of her stressed and bedraggled body.

He tensed as the girls began egging him on. 'Cum in her hard, Daddy, so we can drink from her bitch pussy.' They looked at her, laughing, saying she was so easy to play and so tender.

Crystal begged whomever it was that watched over her dying body that night that they were not the last thing she saw.

Not them fucking laughing at me.

He let out a deep groan as his cum filled her burning tortured insides. The girls ran to the head of the bed, squealing. Elizabeth stroked Crystal's hair back from her face as Georgia look directly in her eyes.

At the same time, Robert Alexander pushed the knife into her chest. She bit hard, almost grateful that he had gagged her. It pierced the skin of her left breast, and then slowly he edged it between her ribs.

She convulsed violently, her bladder giving way as the tip of the blade slid further in.

The two girls were kissing her and screaming high pitched screams of excitement as it penetrated her sad, soft, weak heart and pushed through her sides, blood-spewing and gurgling out.

Her last few moments of life, her last breaths, spent tortured physically and mentally by the faint vision of them lapping up her blood and feasting on her life ebbing away.

Georgia pulled his hot wet cock out of Crystal's dead vagina and began sucking him, loving her taste of death on him. Elizabeth was licking her damaged and torn pussy, not letting any of his cum go to waste.

'Good girls,' he said. 'Daddy is so proud of you both.'

Robert Alexander pushed Georgia on top of Crystal's dead torso, threw her legs apart, and fucked her hard and fast. He was so excited, Crystal's dead body below them, spilling blood with each of his hard thrusts, enjoying the view of her blood splashing, then soaking through the sheets.

Elizabeth was scooping up Crystal's blood and

rubbing it on her and Georgia's bodies and kissed her, sucking her erect nipples.

Daddy pulled out his cock and masturbated, cumming over Georgia's bloody body.

Elizabeth grabbed Daddies cock with her mouth and sucked, drinking his cum while rubbing her hands through the semen and blood covering Georgia's stomach.

CHAPTER 12

He spanked them both and told them to get up and sort out their mess.

Elizabeth, naked and covered in Crystal's coagulated blood, indicated towards a small table covered with a white cloth and all of her belongings on.

'We have everything of hers, except for the phone. But then, Daddy is always so mindful of disposing of the phones... after the distraught messages have been read, of course.'

Both girls giggled and cuddled each other, before Georgia added, 'The cleaners will take care of everything else and will be here in...'

She glanced at the blood-covered watch. '... an hour. Oh, and we mustn't be here when they arrive, Daddy doesn't like us mixing with the cleaners; we are way too special.'

He was admiring them in almost a tender way.

'Daddy is very pleased with you both, but you really must get on - twenty minutes, shower and out.'

CHAPTER 12

They hurried to the bathroom and straight into the shower, washing each other ritualistically and erotically - three times head to toe as he watched them while holding fresh towels. They knew they had to be thorough and scrubbed harder under his scrutiny, taking the towels after being told they had less than five minutes to vacate the penthouse.

Quickly they dressed in their panties and bra, deciding to finish dressing in the lift as there was little time left. They had no intention of not following Daddy's commands. They dare not look back, knowing he liked to spend a little special time with all his conquests.

He and the sad, tortured body of Crystal were all that remained. He made his way to the shower, removing any trace of her. She had almost become repellent to him.

Calmly he dressed in designer elegance as usual and made his way to the lift, checking his reflection and smiling back at himself.

He entered the lift and turned one more time to look upon her, the matted blood-soaked hair and body, and the carnage on the sheets.

'Poor little princess. You sold your soul to me for mortal pleasure. Exist now in the burning fires of hell.'

ACKNOWLEDGMENTS

We would like to thank, jointly, David And Kelly McCaffrey for their continued support and one to one care with our baby – a top top publisher and all round humanists and friend to any that need one.

Personally, I myself, Gabriella, would like to thank Kerry Foyle for her continued friendship and support – she really is a top girl!

And also Sarah Mackbride who we hope to see back soon… she is sorely missed…

ABOUT THE AUTHOR

Bella Donna (real name Donna Marie McCarthy… shhhh), is the author of gothic horror titles, Alma Mater, Biddy Trott, The Meddler and The Hangman's Hitch

Robert Alexander is the author of many dark works soon to be published here …

Printed in Great Britain
by Amazon